Rags to Bollywood

'A Bollywood film in a book! – amazing!!'

Sonny Singh Kalar

www.masalabooks.com   masalabooks@yahoo.com

Grosvenor House
Publishing Limited

All rights reserved
Copyright © Sonny Singh Kalar, 2009

Sonny Singh Kalar is hereby identified as author of this
work in accordance with Section 77 of the Copyright, Designs
and Patents Act 1988

The book cover picture is copyright to Sonny Singh Kalar

This book is published by
Grosvenor House Publishing Ltd
28-30 High Street, Guildford, Surrey, GU1 3HY.
www.grosvenorhousepublishing.co.uk

This book is sold subject to the conditions that it shall not, by way of
trade or otherwise, be lent, resold, hired out or otherwise circulated
without the author's or publisher's prior consent in any form of binding or
cover other than that in which it is published and
without a similar condition including this condition being imposed
on the subsequent purchaser.

A CIP record for this book
is available from the British Library

ISBN 978-1-906645-97-7

Dedicated to 'Dylan'
You have my every confidence and I love you more than life itself...

A note from the author...

Life never stops moving — Neither should you!"

Welcome to the magic of 'Masala Books' and the splendour of the written word in all its grisly glory. Buckle up and prepare to be thrust into a land that knows no bounds. Remember that a tree is truly judged by the quality of its fruit. I hope that you find this fruity third book in the 'Masala Books' range just the edifying aphrodisiac you need to intoxicate and pep up your days.

When you are feeling blue just remember that life isn't all sunshine and chocolates, it as near to perfect as you can achieve at any given time. It is human nature to aspire for an even better life and this is why it is imperative that you seek out your dreams and reach for the sky. By making big plans you stir your heart. As was once said, if you aim for the ceiling, you may reach it, aim for the sky and you never know. Don't forget to hold your head up high as you stroll through the playground of despair, for you roll the dice to your own future.

When the chips have fallen and the sun sets;

Live each day as though it is your last crazy day on this sprawling metropolis,
Sing like no-one can hear you,
Dance like no-one is watching,
Live for the pleasure of life and not just for the toil,
Blub like a baby when watching a mushy film,
Laugh aloud and laugh often,
Then after all that, run like mad from the men in white coats when they come looking for you with dog catcher nets.
Lastly, if nothing else, make buying 'Masala Books' your ultimate passion in life (wink).
You can only ever do your best with what you have!
Best of luck and remember to love and cherish those in your inner circle of trust...

Sonny Singh Kalar - *a cat on his own path...and here to add some passion to your reading...*

Catch the other great titles in the Masala Book range
from
Sonny Singh Kalar;

Masala Wedding

Naughty Indian Affairs

Contents

Chapter 1	Painful Day's of Yore	1
Chapter 2	Dream the Dream	17
Chapter 3	Crunch Time	31
Chapter 4	Human Faeces Detector	41
Chapter 5	Hasta Luego Amigo	51
Chapter 6	Viva La India	61
Chapter 7	Mumbai Dangerous	79
Chapter 8	A Taste of Bollywood	88
Chapter 9	Wolf at the Door	99
Chapter 10	Actor's Paradise	108
Chapter 11	The Bionic Swami	121
Chapter 12	Hunger Pangs	131
Chapter 13	Reflective Fortitude	139
Chapter 14	Smokescreen	144
Chapter 15	Bloodbath at the 'Mumbai Coral'	154
Chapter 16	'Roofies' Delight	164
Chapter 17	Perilous Sign	171
Chapter 18	Hidden Treasure	176
Chapter 19	Judgement Day	182
Chapter 20	Knock Knock	192
Chapter 21	There is no Sacrifice	204
Chapter 22	I can't believe it is not butter	210
Chapter 23	Lucidity and Veracity – Brother's in Arms	218
Chapter 24	Pincer Movement	228
Chapter 25	The Final Resolution	234

Chapter 1

Painful day's of yore

'Your life is written for you and the course of destiny cannot be changed'

THOSE HALCYON DAYS GROWING UP...

'Sam, you bastard,' he shouted from across the road. The local bully had reacted to seeing me that day. His jaundiced comment and flagrant disregard for my feelings was so lucidly evident in his hostility. The words sledge hammered home, like the proverbial dagger through the heart. I had been called that before when I was growing up, but it never carried as much veracity and brutal realisation as it did on that day. The cut throat malignance and balefulness those few words conveyed, sliced deep into the very bowels of my body. Despite all of his frailties, the truth of the matter was that he was right - I was a true bastard.

Mum and dad had perished some years before in a tragic car accident. They had been decapitated and their cleanly severed heads lying in the back seat of their mangled up car had offered some credibility to their absolute demise. A horrific, torturous, and debilitating scene of sheer carnage that rocked my foundations with meteoric force, and one that uncle had so graphically informed me about in the years gone by. It was certainly in keeping with his overall sadistic nature and mannerisms. I never got to say goodbye, but then I did not know what karma had in store for them that fateful day when I traipsed off to school as a young ten year old, whilst my parents went about their daily business. Such harrowing anguish and torment has kept me awake many, many times. I have harassed and agonised over why I had to suffer such a cruel and merciless blow, but the answer always remained the same and that was they were gone – forever.

It was a moment when I wished I could have hit the back button as you do on a computer and restored parity back to my life. The very thought that those of us who have loved and lost have wished for many times in those dark moments of yearning when the saucer sized tears have fallen.

Once you have experienced a grief and seen how it resonates around you, piercing through your soul, flickering around you like a burning maelstrom of fire, a halo of hurt and thorns of real tangible pain. The feeling of wishing and yearning to see your loved one's just once more, to touch their soft cheeks and to hear their dulcet tones. I had loved hard and without compromise, but this only made things worse. I cherished those moments with every single vestige of happiness and fulfilment that I could muster, for those fleeting moments were gone in a whim, never to return.

Life is full of snares, heartache and intangible obstacles and I quickly started to realize that to get anything in this world you had to be ruthless, a modern day snake charmer and cut throat merchant to get what you were owed by others and society. This was the lesson that life had taught me through those turbulent years after the loss of my nearest and dearest.

Since that day to this, I have the scars to back up what I am telling you, as they say I am long in the tooth, so old I've even grown whiskers. I once heard somewhere that to beat the players, you have to be a player, but what do you do when life has kicked you in the ghoulies from the earliest age, and then even pissed on you as you writhe around on the ground. Staying one step ahead, being smart, being shrewd, outfoxing your enemies and never letting your guard down, even when in the company of friends, this was the name of the game and basic survival instinct that I tried to use as a moral compass in my formative years. Anyway, I talk a good fight, but where did it ever get me? The path to my destiny has been painful and convoluted and this is where my story begins, warts and all…

Growing up as a white lad in the depths of Slough was a blast, dad was great, a big, tall, strong husk of a man. He was like a modern day Spartan, and my mum's very own John Wayne. He would sometimes pick me up with one hand and dangle me like a rag doll, just to show off his impressive strength. There were so many happy memories with them both, with mum the softer and more genteel of the two, she was quiet and unassuming but liked the fact that her man was there to look after her, well until that one day when their car skidded under the lorry, until that sorrowful day…

In moments that I will cherish forever, I recall how mum and dad would tell me stories about how I would achieve great things in my life. They were very superstitious and would often visit fortune tellers and Indian pundits to have my 'teva' (unique future horoscope) read and written out for me to use as a kind of map for my life.

Our long standing family friends were an Indian family – the Agarwal's and lived several streets away from us in my home town of Slough. My best friend Dalj, who was of similar age to me, was their only son and I truly respected them as a family. They were devoted and genuinely nice people. Dalj's father and my dad's friend was Karpal Singh Agarwal, a smart traditional Sikh guy, with his immaculately groomed array of turbans, some the size of ufo's, that he donned whenever we saw him. His loyalty and devotion to his family was unequalled and he simply oozed faithfulness within his inner circle. He was the one who had introduced my dad to the 'teva' readings and took him to a couple of haunts where this practice went on. Over the years, I had come to realise that there are a lot of gullible people out there who sheepishly follow these mystical pundits like they are some kind of demi-Gods. I could appreciate that there were certainly a handful who were genuine and were able to sprinkle their magic into your life, whether this was the feel good placebo factor, the X factor or just having more attuned chakra's then the average person is anyone's guess. (The chakra, referred to the third eye on your forehead, rather like a spiritual Cyclops). Then there were the money spinning stage coach robbers, the one's who would ask you to close your eyes so that you could indulge in that transcendent and meditative state. This would then enable them to rifle through your belongings, nicking your 'green' and quickly checking out your personal details so that they could then mystically drop them into conversation when they began their 'spiritual reading.'

It is a sad and tragic state of affairs but this was what I was seeing when I was growing up. You would see the vast adverts plastered all over the backs of daily rags with their resplendent and unfortunately enticing words luring the suckers in society into their web of conniving deceit. I knew this and kept my guard up even though I was as innocent as the day was long.

Many traditional Punjabi folk absolutely swore by these 'teva' and in many cases, depending on the source the 'teva' was obtained from, i.e. the genuine guys out there, some of the predictions were coincidentally but yet unnervingly accurate, and thus the entire mythology and belief system of their powers was born.

One day dad actually showed me the Holy Grail, my 'teva.' There it was in the palm of his hand with smoke bellowing out from the papers, not really, but it might as well have been such was the drum rolling significance of it. This was the golden egg and he went through it with me word for word and told me in graphic detail what cards destiny held for me.

Dad spoke, 'Son, it says that you will make it in life and be very successful, but only if you remain cautious of treacherous people. You will need to be one step ahead at all times. It talks of shrewdness, being smart and watching people closely, closer than you need to!'

One step ahead, I had no idea what he was talking about but listened on nevertheless.

Dad continued, 'The teva has been written by a swami deep in the forest's of India when the Agarwal's visited last year. I asked them to have your reading done. All he needed was your date of birth, your name and that was it.'

This was strange when I thought that some orange robed swami had been sweating over my horoscope last year. It must have been the very first white 'teva' reading he had performed, and even at ten years old and despite wearing the goofiest expression this side of town, I smelt a dirty stinking rat, but went along with it.

'Yes son it goes on to say that there will be a life changing event for you very soon, something that will devastate you, but you will soon recover and then you will seek your dream immediately after this event. This dream and path in life will be what you are destined to do. Only then will you be healthy and successful, but remember, treachery is only a heartbeat away – be safe, be warned and above all be alive!'

I was astounded. What fricking pills was this god damn swami consuming? The guy had written war and peace I thought at the time. He was wasting his talents skulking in the wilderness of India. This dude should have been signed up for his own live chat show with his adept artistic talents shining through in such carefully constructed prose.

However, in subsequent years the relevance of those chilling words came crushing home to rip my heart out. The day the news was delivered to me during English class will remain with me forever. Their fate had been written through my reading and not even they knew the chilling thought that on that very day when dad had read my 'teva', he was in actual fact holding his very own death warrant in his hands – destiny awaited them.

Things happened quickly after that life shattering day, the funeral arrangements were taken care of by my dad's younger brother, uncle Terry and his wife auntie Myleene. My parent's house was sold and the legal paperwork including my custody was dealt with amongst other matters.

The only things I recollect through the haziness of it all was hearing the solicitor mumble something about a will reading, about the entire estate, life insurances and other pension type contributions all being paid to me on my eighteenth birthday, and not a dime was to be paid to me sooner than that.

It all felt surreal, I simply sat back and let my uncle and auntie take care of the arrangements, they knew what they were doing after all. They lived on our street too so moving in with them was a no brainer. I knew that I would carry the loss as a heavy hearted burden for the rest of my days. It was inevitable.

As time progressed, I noticed a sweeping change in uncle Terry and auntie Myleene. Their attitude and mannerisms towards me became increasingly more and more hostile. It was now that the cracks in my relationship with them were beginning to seep through. They resented me and I would even say despised me judging by the hostilities that were meted out to me in a myriad of cringing moments.

They were a different breed entirely, unscrupulous and utterly amoral, and I would often wonder if they had in fact been swapped at birth in a secret hospital somewhere with their real mothers being jackals. These apostles of Satan had for some reason set out to make my life a total misery in the weeks after my parent's funeral. They would hit me for no reason, lock me in my bedroom, or ground me for what felt like an eternity. They were control freaks and when I went to school, uncle would chastise me for being five minutes late. I lived in fear and knew that a cold hearted lashing was never far away when these pestiferous goons were nearby.

Auntie Myleene was a sadist of Nazi Germany ilk and possessed as much charisma and magnetism as a dead fish. She would have been chief commander in the Gestapo such was her ruthless streak I tell you. I still have the scars to prove that she was definitely a degree holder in accurate striking - when she swung, she scored.

She was like the Babe Ruth of newspaper swatting, a national pastime where budding housewives would attempt to crush the fragile skulls of young orphaned adolescents for not tidying up the mess in their bedrooms.

She would never need an excuse to bash me unceremoniously. I mean I feared at times she would even plant things in my bedroom and then set about beating me to within one inch of my life just to flex her muscles and keep me in check. Then, there was the alcohol, the crates upon crates of booze flowing down their gullets on an almost incomparable scale. They drank and smelled like stinking fish, quaffing can after can of cheap ale as a habitual routine.

My life was a total disaster movie being played out before me and there was no escape.

Uncle was a drunkard, nothing more and nothing less. His preferred method of torture was tying me up as a young boy and setting about me with sharp implements. He would use this tactic several times a week to instil lamb like fear in me and to let me know that he was 'El Queso Grande' of the house.

One horrific example springs to mind. It had been a few years since the memory of my parents had been hauntingly fading. I had been living with them for a while now and the abuse had exacerbated. This day, he stood there with little dribbles of foam forming on the sides of his mouth. He was drunkenly swaying his portly frame with his pot belly protruding over his trousers.

'Why are you doing this?' I pleaded. I sat there trussed up in my bedroom, tied up with rope and with no hope of escape, with the rope wound so tightly that my wrists began to bleed.

'You need to be taught a lesson, and my boy this is the only way you will learn,' he snarled back at me. He was more than braced to deal me an indiscriminate and savage bite and his obvious venom and evident disdain was bursting out of every facial aperture.

My ever burgeoning fear merely adding to his lustre, and at that moment I succumbed to the anguishing tenet that he would remain as evil, unchanged and unrepentant for as long as the blood of the Devil coursed through his veins.

With that, he lowered the blade down past the incriminating stain that had now appeared in the crotch of my lightly coloured jeans and flicked it a few times slashing up at my chest in his drunken stupor. I knew that I would be extremely fortunate to survive this encounter without some form of physical abuse, as had been the case for the past few years, well as far back as I could remember.

I saw the serrated tip of the butcher's knife inching its way menacingly towards my eyes, the fierce and brutal realisation that my destiny was being played out before me. I closed my eyes, today was a good day to die. At least now, I would be emancipated from a life of hate and torment.

My executioner sized me up, to him I was a waste of skin and sinew, the shit off his shoe and a worm he was just itching to dispirit and crush. Why did he despise me so much? The pallor of death carved on my face did nothing to assuage his determined bullying and forthcoming onslaught of violence. The quivering lip was merely fuel for his burning fire of evil and did nothing to slake his intentions of eviscerating me without compunction or passion.

The village drunkard and troublemaker swayed from side to side as he tightened the grip on the knife. There were more slashes along with accompanying bile filled abuse, more jabbing with his finger and even more expletives, when suddenly the demented creature lunged forward taking a firm grip of my hair in his tightly woven fist causing me to yelp like a distressed puppy. The unexpectedness of the grab was quickly followed by a swishing noise above my head and then raucous laughing, the searing pain shooting to my brain.

Time stood still momentarily as my mind attempted to comprehend what had just occurred. I held my breath. What was happening here? My head was dizzy with shock and an equal amount of loathing, my eyes unable to focus in the darkness.

Suddenly the door opened and auntie Myleene flicked the light on.

'There, now go to your gungadin acting classes with your paki mates,' uncle hissed as he dangled a fistful of my hair in front of me.

'What have you done? What have you done to me? I stuttered and repeated, disconsolately and utterly shocked.

He had hacked off a clump of my hair and paraded it to me like a trophy depicting his insane iniquity. What was wrong with him? How could he have done this to me? I grappled with the thought of resembling Kojak for the next few months as he tossed the clump of my hair on the floor. It was a defining moment that consolidated my hatred for him, a moment when he dropped straight out of the love category as far as I was concerned.

Myleene exchanged a concerned look as she quickly set about trying to untie me from the tightly woven rope around my body before they both exited the room. This was one occasion when I somehow survived an unprovoked onslaught from auntie, maybe even she was shocked by the sickening assault she had walked in on. I lay asleep that night several years ago, soaking my pillow with tears of yearning for my parents. How I missed them and how I loved them so much. They would never have stood for anyone treating me in this appalling manner - that was for sure.

I prayed and cried myself to sleep reflecting on my crime, wanting to make something of my life and training to be an actor at Grooving Singh's Drama School and that was all. A life long ambition that had followed me throughout my childhood ever since Dalj had exposed me to some great Bollywood movies.

For years the gruesome twosome had been slowly sucking the life force out of me and standing in the way of me fulfilling the one last granule of hope that I had in my life and that was to galvanise my existence into something that my real parents looking down on me would be proud of.

Their motivation and vindictive nature towards me was baffling. I felt as though they resented the fact that they could never have children. I had overheard something about auntie having rotten eggs and uncle not having enough juice in the tank. They also detested the fact that I had now been foisted upon them in such dramatic fashion and the fact that they had not yet seen a penny of the inheritance that had been left for me in my parent's will. My gratis existence got up their noses and this was their way of making me pay for it, I became the punch-bag for all their ills in life, the situation was as bleak as that.

If all that wasn't bad enough I also had to contend with the habitual grunting and groaning of auntie Myleene as she was rogered to what sounded like an inch of her life by the rampant sex pest that Terry had become once he allowed the fifteen gallons of booze swishing in his 'Fatty McFatkins' stomach to dictate his moods.

His portly 'Blubberdale' body a perfect advert depicting a life of over indulgent boozing, smoking and scoffing his face with full English breakfasts or heart attacks on a plate. He was literally one fry up away from the cardiology department but he did not care a tiny rat's arse about that. Their booze fuelled, chandelier swinging nookie brought on my pains with capitulating disgust on an almost daily basis.

Terry smacked of the type of reprehensible creature who would take with one hand and not bother giving back with the other, the unkempt, wretched and selfish slime ball who would wash their hands before they went for a dump and not after, proving that they cared only for themselves and not a shit about anyone else. He was a dog!

I just had to get out of the house at any given opportunity. The atmosphere was depressing and bringing me down so much that I felt like curling up into a ball and dying on an almost daily basis. Life simply did not become more soul destroying than this. How many times can someone be told that they are useless and that they will amount to nothing?

I would often cry myself to sleep in those formative years. They say that struggle is the father of all things, and that there was always some hope around the corner, but this was scant consolation because I still walked around with an unrivalled feeling of emptiness. In these times, I sought solace in the escapism of my acting. I had been going ever since I was younger and could save up enough money from my paper rounds, odd jobs and crucially getting mini loans from my drama school friends.

One particular friend was Anil, a friend who unfortunately after lending me so much in fees got in with the wrong crowd and then dramatically left the school to be a gangster and drugs czar. It was a waste of such a precocious talent, but he had chosen his path and that was that. My years at drama school had been the most exciting of my life. It was where I felt I belonged and could live, breathe and truly exist.

My teacher – Visperal Canchita often commented that I had the makings of a true star one day especially if I continued to act as I had been. These kinds of edifying and soothing words meant everything to me, absolutely the world, and I was eternally grateful.

I was about to turn eighteen and on the cusp of receiving over two hundred and fifty thousand pounds from all of the various life insurances and other monetary assets left in my parent's will. The money meant nothing to me and in actual fact, I couldn't really have cared less about it. However it was coming to me whether I wanted it or not and so I had arranged with my bank manager to take ownership within a few days.

I had hoped to keep this inheritance a secret but uncle Terry with his fog horn mouth had for the past years told everyone within the community, friends, family, the milkman and even the local cat. There were people in comas in the local hospital who knew all about the money. Word spread like wild fire and this in itself manifested many awkward and problematic situations with people that I met.

It seemed everyone, including uncle and auntie were after a slice of the wedge no matter what the odds. It put me on my guard most of the time, well until I could clearly establish someone's motivation for wanting to know me. They say that loose words at any time always equated to long term damage, a thought that worried me many times over the years. I was fully aware that money was the root of all evil and if history and the experiences of great men before me had told me anything, it was that money made people do the most outrageous things and it was something for me to ponder in quieter moments.

Monday 6th July - On this particular day just under two weeks ago, I had returned home to the usual barrage of questions and expletives from the pair of them before slinking off to my room for some rest. I lay back on the bed, my eyes heavy and soul weary. The thoughts of some great drama scenes that I had acted out that evening percolated in my mind as I found myself drifting off, huddled up into a ball and deep in slumberous Slumbers Ville.

Suddenly I woke with a startle and there was the moment of magic, the epiphany in my life. I saw the figure of a tall man, devilishly handsome, oozing gravitas and a magical aura. At first his face was covered in a magical white mist and as the mist slowly cleared the ghostly figure revealed himself to me…it was my dad. He was so real I could actually smell him. I looked on in amazement.

He stood there looking down at me as I lay there rubbing my eyes.

'Sam, you are a wonderful boy and if you want to see what you can become in life, then follow your heart and pursue your dreams. Your destiny awaits.' His words sounded magical and surreal. I wept like a baby. I was mesmerised, truly awestruck. I quickly checked the bed side table for signs of empty vodka and rum bottles to ensure that this was not some delusional alcoholic hallucination that I was having, but the table stared back at me completely booze free.

'Son, it is written that you will be great one day and I promise you soon everything will become clear to you – everything about life!' He was succinct and it was a deeply coded message amidst the mayhem of my life up until that point.

'But how?' I asked quickly.

The misty apparition of dad laughed heartily and then like a puff of smoke…he was gone.

I lay there stunned; this was the best moment of my life – ever!

I had to tell Dalj and my girlfriend Prity all about it. I couldn't wait and lay awake the whole night staring into the empty void where dad had appeared. They would never believe me I thought as my heart filled with happiness and hope for the future.

Why he had come to visit me was beyond my field of knowledge, but the huge, shiny tears that were streaming down my cheeks suddenly gave my disjointed existence some real purpose and meaning.

My 'teva' and formal roadmap to success was now once again at the forefront of my mind and it was just unfathomable. What precarious and pit fallen road would his advice take me down? What I had not realised at the time was that a whole can of deadly worms had just been let out and my spirit was about to embark upon the most dangerous but unforgettable mission, where there was to be no guarantee that I would ever come back alive!

Chapter 2

Dream the dream

Tuesday 7th July – All I ever wanted was to be an actor and my life had been a work in progress since I was a child. It was the dream of this lifelong goal that had spurred me on. It kept me safe from the jaws of despair on many occasions and essentially prevented me from cracking up. The salvaging belief that there just could be something bigger and better out there was a hope that I simply could not relinquish.

I sat in my room on the phone to Dalj, my close confidant. In the background, a collection of Bhangra tracks from a CD that Dalj had lent me a few years ago were playing. When I had first started to listen to this music I could not understand a word of what was being sung, but the cheerful melodies helped me escape the spiralling thoughts of despair that often churned through my mind when I was banished to my room, nigh on every day. However, with time spent at Grooving Singh's Drama School along with Dalj's regular input I became quite proficient in Hindi and Punjabi and for a white guy was very proud of that fact. Dalj had even shown me the light bulb screwing dance, the whisky bottle on the head jive and not forgetting the hoi hoi dance when you thrust your foot in and out of the circle – like the Punjabi hokey cokey - I simply loved them. However, he reserved the best until last - the 'pendu' or 'freshie dance' as he referred to it. This was when he would stand on the spot doing a double light bulb screwing move with his hands up above him and with one leg up to knee height jumping off the ground continuously, all this with an accompanying grin that would have put the Cheshire Cat out of business. Dalj was a legend to me, a true and honourable friend, one who would be a mere phone call away to help while away my troubles and heartache at any given hour. He always knew what to say and when to say it, hell the guy could have been my brother. Our friendship had been built on the foundation of trust and understanding. I had even told him about Terry and Myleene and I could tell that he vicariously felt my turmoil just from the reaction on his face.

I remained on the phone with Dalj while Terry and Myleene were sat downstairs in the living room. They had already been at the sauce ever since I had returned from University some hours before.

'Sam, come on over. Mum has cooked up some lovely food and there is plenty for you here mate,' Dalj politely offered.

'Oh nice, thanks! Mate I have to tell you something unbelievable that happened last night' I said.

'Cool, tell me when you get here. So you coming over?' he asked.

'Yeah I'll see you in ten minutes. I have got to get past the two sentries downstairs first.' I replied nervously.

As I terminated the call, I could hear the clinking of glasses from below as the merriment continued. I could hear the incessant chatter and the kind of putting the world to right speeches that all alcoholics engage in when sozzled as newts. This was interspersed with sporadic raucous laughter, sloppy and slurpy kissing as they sat in paralytic inebriation getting more and more drunk by the minute.

Their loutish behaviour often made my toes curl in embarrassment and only the smothering of my pillow over my head and cranking up of the Bhangra CD were small crumbs of comfort that I could cling on to.

I had never had any input in the day to day running of the house and any dreams and ideas that I drummed up were always squashed like the bugs they were. In a sentence, it felt as though I was in the way of their lifestyle and they would have preferred me dead, well not around in any case.

Right now, I got myself ready and crept down the stairs, past the living room where the slurps were frighteningly loud and I somehow managed to sneak out of the door like a stealthy Ninja without alerting the pair of inhumane Rottweiler's lurking in close proximity. I had made it and was free for the evening and hastily scuttled my way over to Dalj's house a few streets away. It was eight in the evening and this part of Slough was a relatively quiet and leafy area. My biggest concern was probably worrying about being mugged by a gang of gun toting field mice armed with sharpened blades of grass than anything more deadly such was the tangible tranquillity on the streets, unlike other parts of Slough where you would be mugged for your teeth or bad breath let alone anything else.

Over the years I would often conjure up excuses to pop over to see him and his family, they always made me feel so welcome. His mum Saraswati was so wonderful and everything auntie was not, her cooking was from another planet – Planet cordon bleu. She was a true gastronome genius and such a sweet natured person. The only thing missing was the halo nestling on her head. Her culinary paradise of herbs and spices, not to mention succulent curries wafting throughout the house like the Bisto advert always buckled my knees whenever I set foot through the door. She nailed it every time and I had a smile bigger than The Joker when I prepared to sink my fangs into her dishes of delight.

Dalj opened the door and led me inside to the living room. Saraswati said hello as she beavered away in the kitchen like a possessed chef, whilst his dad Karpal sat on the sofa watching some sort of Bollywood movie on the box. We would all often reminisce about my parents and as true family friends they understood my plight. I remember Karpal even offering to adopt me in the aftermath, but this was not to be as Terry stamped his marker down long before and had made the decision.

The hospitality that I received whenever I walked into their den of nirvana almost brought me to tears each and every time. But, on this occasion I managed to refrain from crying as Dalj guided me to the dining table where he quickly began to scoop various curries and dishes into my stainless steel plate, one with at least six small compartments for different types of food to be housed – ingenious. I was starving and the slice of toast I had consumed earlier as my evening meal at home did not quite fill me up.

I was so grateful and actually got told off by Saraswati for saying thank you about thirty four times in a minute, I am sorry but I was just not used to it, this felt more home to me then anything I had ever been exposed to.

Sitting at the far end of the room was Pinto. She was Dalj's gran and a small squat lady who for some reason always wore a white Asian suit and white headscarf or chunni as it was referred to by Dalj.

We all called her dadiji, which meant gran. I was told that we had to stick on the 'ji' bit at the end of 'dadi' when addressing people of her stature as a term of endearment. This demonstrated your respect and acknowledgement of their omnipotence.

She was knocking on a bit and at around sixty five years of age, she was technically the head of the house as would be expected being Karpal's mum. Karpal's dad and Pinto's other half had passed away naturally some time before. Pinto had always been a staunch advocate of tranquillity and displayed effective leadership qualities for her generation. Well, that was until a few years ago when for some bizarre reason she went bonkers and lost the plot. She was the quintessential March Hare, bells and whistles too. Before then I had noticed an ever burgeoning state of insanity seeping through. One time Dalj and I even caught her standing on a chair in the kitchen one day after school, licking bits of paper and sticking them to her face before trying to blow them off with her mouth. Other times she would come hurtling out of the kitchen armed with the broom chasing imaginary mice from the kitchen and out into the street. She would sometimes even get to the end of the road screaming like a banshee with the broom held above her head like some kind of Zulu warrior. It would often take a monumental tussle just to get her back in the confines of the house and convince her that we were not being over run by killer mice. The neighbours often gave her quizzical looks when they saw her out in the front garden on her own. She had slowly turned into a raving lunatic which meant all of the Agarwal's and myself included were on dadiji sentry duties more frequently than not. Dalj would often phone me in the evening breathing a huge sigh of relief when the old buzzard hit the sack and the land of the zzz's. She was slowly becoming the problem in everyone's life and it seemed was in need of a good break to get the sun on her wrinkled back and to invigorate her one worn and bruised brain cell floating around helplessly within her skull.

I waved hello to dadiji Pinto and she flashed a toothless grin back at me as she rocked back and forth at electrifying speed on the sofa, her soggy dentures laying on the arm support next to her and white chunni flapping uncontrollably around her head. It was as though she was about to take off such was the ferocity of her rocking as she sat in her own bubble of madness.

'Tuck in mate, the food is fresh.' Dalj pointed to my brimming steel tray.

Without a second's remorse I tucked into the dishes and attacked the chappati's like a down and out vagrant, the only thing missing was the bad hair do, green finger nails and smell of wee.

'Sam, you will love this guy.' Dalj pointed to the TV screen in the living room. I looked over, my mouth stuffed to the brim with chapatti, a strange green dish or 'saag' as Dalj described it and some chicken pieces. I could see a Bollywood actor standing on a stage and singing to an audience. He was belting out a mushy ballard and seemingly captivated those around him who were listening, including Dalj's family.

Dalj left the table to watch, moving into the living room and I found myself joining him leaving my food behind. We stood there watching as Dalj explained that he was a guy called Amitabh Bacchan and it was a classic song from a film called Mukkader Ka Sikkander, one that I had not seen as yet.

He then proceeded to tell me that he was singing the song to his childhood sweetheart and he was remembering the times when he was growing up with her beside him and how hard his life had been thus far, this was shown through a series of flashbacks. He told me that the fly in the ointment was that the girl who was also watching him on the stage actually loved someone else, his best friend and this consolidated his pain. He elaborated and told me that in his role throughout the film, his character was treated like dirt by everyone, and despite this anguish, he still sacrificed his love and everything he had for those he cared for. I immediately sensed the parallels to my life; it was palpable.

I found myself crying, the tears slowly meandering their way down my cheeks and a strange knot tightening in my stomach. It was at that moment of divine clarity that everything in my life made sense. The acting that I was witnessing was so amazingly touching and moving that I found myself staring in open mouthed shock. I loved him with passion and his role in the film was so easy to relate to. His eyes told of a story of devotion and sacrifice, and I had never seen acting so dramatic and mesmerising in any film. The power and magnificence of his performance was all consuming. Destiny had just rubber stamped itself squarely on my forehead on this very day. I knew that I needed to be sedulous in my dream of being an actor, just to emulate a fraction of what substance that this legend portrayed.

Dalj told me that he was revered as a God by people from all walks of life and from all over the world. This guy had become an instant hero in my life, a role model who I had been searching for an eternity. He was the ray of light that I needed to fill the gaping wound that had been my life as far back as I could remember. He was my reason for living in that single watershed moment and my mind was transfixed on this legendary performer. After the song had finished I grabbed Dalj and told him to tell me everything about this great actor. The next two hours we sat in his room and he sung like a canary, answering all the questions like his life depended on it. It was as though he was on an episode of Mastermind with his specialist subject -'Amitabh Bacchan.'

During my frenzied interrogation of Dalj's knowledge and test of will power, I could see the shepherds crook appearing from the side of the room ready to grab me around the throat and yank me off before Dalj started dousing himself in petrol or hurling himself out of the window.

Despite my over flowing enthusiasm, Dalj like the steadfast friend he was had nailed it and giving me all the ammunition I needed to follow in the footsteps of this divine inspiration in my flaky and rudderless life. This was when I discovered the meaning of friendship, when I discovered life and more importantly when I met the most revered and amazing Indian actor ever to have graced the earth. The man not only acted, he owned the stage and actually brought a ray of sunshine to my disconsolate existence, a man who changed my life forever.

At that exact moment and in a moment of startling serendipity my mobile started to ring in my pocket and I moved to one side and answered it.

It was Visperal Canchita, my drama teacher, 'Sam, I have some great news for you, great news!' He purred.

'What's happened?' I asked.

'You have got your break, you have been selected to go to India next week to visit the Bollywood film industry in Mumbai and audition for a part in a big movie, called 'The Valati' (meaning the foreigner and where the word Blighty originated from). My friend you will be hooked up with an agent who will show you around out there. How does that sound?'

I almost collapsed such was the electricity shooting through my body. This was surreal. I had my break, it was happening. 'Are you sure?' I asked desperately.

'Never been more sure. I have just posted you the details, so keep a look out in the post.'

After I terminated the call I felt elated. The earlier predictions in my life were all coming to life. The visit, the break, it was all too good to be true. I felt like jumping up in the air and strumming the air guitar with unrestricted ebullience.

'What's happened? Dalj asked enthusiastically.

'I have done it. I have got a break in Bollywood, yesssss!' I punched the air with delight and for some bizarre reason broke out into the finest Bhangra moves this side of town joined by an equally jubilant Dalj. He cranked up the stereo and we danced like madmen for a few minutes busting all kinds of Punjabi moves such was the adrenaline shooting through our bodies upon hearing the news.

I was travelling to the pulsating city of Mumbai, the pearl of the East, a vibrant, heart stopping gem of a city and one that I had been told before never sleeps.

'That is crazy, first your dad told you about this kind of thing happening and then you get a visit and now this. Mate this is your destiny right here.' Dalj was as positive as he always was and his input was crucial.

'I am in shock!' I stuttered.

'Yeah, well you have got good acting skills. You have all the certificates and trophies from the drama school and not to mention you have got a bank balance that would make most people whimper with full access to that money in a few days hey.'

I stopped dancing and looked at him for a moment and then to the floor, the cogs churned around in my head, something just wasn't right.

'Yeah. I know. Hang on…I never told you that I get that money when I am eighteen…err…how do you know that mate?' I was left slightly confused as I had made it a point not to gloat or even discuss my financial windfall to anyone. Even though as much as I trusted Dalj, I always felt that this was not money that I had earned or anything but was a painful reminder that it replaced the once doting parents that I had.

Dalj suddenly appeared flustered and even though he had nut brown skin, he actually started to go red in the face. He remained silent.

'Mate, what's the matter. I am just asking how you found out that is all. I don't mean it in a bad way or anything.' I reassured him but kept my reservations for the time deeply suppressed.

'Nah I just heard stuff that is all.'

'What stuff?'

'That…that you have got a quarter of a million pounds coming to you when you reach eighteen.'

'For the last time...MATE...who told you?' I stood up and stared down at him, my internal dialogue feeding me all kinds of suspicious and unfriendly suggestions as to his motives. There was something not right about the whole situation. What was going on? Maybe I was just being hard on him unnecessarily, but I was becoming fed up of people thinking that I was obtuse and had a shining red squeaky nose. I scrutinised his face after taking off my donkey ears and placing them on the table beside me.

Dalj paused and stood up slowly, 'Look I overheard Terry talking about it one day with Myleene, and he...'

'He said what?' I interrupted him.

'He said to her that once they get your money then they will kick you out of the house. Dalj looked convincing with his explanation. He continued, 'She even talked about, you know...getting rid of you somehow.'

I staggered back and sat on the bed, at best his actions were incompetent. I was incredulous and appalled at what I had just heard. Was Dalj telling the truth or was he hiding something from me?

'I think that they may have killed before mate, so you have to watch your back.' Dalj's words carried an air of frightening caution.

'What killed before...you mean,' the words stuck in my throat, 'Even their own family members?'

'That is exactly what I mean.' Dalj snapped back at me. He had a determined look on his face.

He had mentioned this before to me in the past but I always treated his assessment with the contempt it deserved and disregarded the sinister thoughts. They were simply not capable of killing, it was not in our family bloodline. Despite this, my mind was still jumbled up and I knew that I had to escape for my own sanity let alone anything else. There was a part of me not sitting comfortably with what had occurred this evening as I trudged off home. The only thing that was guaranteed was that I had discovered my new found path in life. Destiny had curled its finger up and beckoned me to Bollywood. This was my chance to fuse East and West and become a success in the Bollywood film industry and I was determined that nobody was going to stand in my way.

On my walk back to the house I called my girlfriend Prity. She was a lovely girl, full of bounce and with unbridled love for me. Our meeting had been fated last year when she bumped me in the University canteen and knocked my plate of food out of my hand and across the floor. I had never seen someone panic and worry as much as she did, I remember how she persistently said sorry, and had blamed it on the time of the month, her being dizzy and clumsy amongst other things. I just stared at how beautiful she looked as she babbled on whilst attempting to scoop up the remnants of my food back into the plate. Call me old fashioned but I kind of went off my food after that as the thought of eating a piece of fish laced with chewing gum and fluff didn't quite appeal anymore. After that moment she promised to buy me coffee whilst still apologising profusely and then we hit it off and soon afterwards became an item.

She was like a ray of sunshine in my life and that was probably the best accidental bump that I could ever have hoped for, because as I knew full well, had it not been for that we would never have met, as she was way out of my league.

On the phone I explained what had happened last night with the visit from dad, and then told her about the phone-call and my plans about visiting Bollywood.

'Babes, like I have said before, you should go for it. I will always be there for you, you know that.' Her dulcet tones the perfect aphrodisiac for my ears.

'You think so? What about us? I can't leave you here.' I had not thought it through as the realisation of time apart did not appeal.

'Do you really want this?' she asked.

'Of course I do, but I want you more.' I replied quick as a bolt.

'Then life is about sacrifice, about following your dreams. Who am I to stand in your way? Her response was beginning to terrify me.

'No, Prity wait...'

'Look I know how important it is for you, so...I will go with you?'

'You would do that?' I asked with my heart swelling with contentment.

'I would do anything for you. I am prepared to go with you to India okay. Let's go and roll the dice and see where it lands.' She was the sporran in my life, a magical person and it felt as though the words flowed through the mobile phone like poetry.

I walked through the gate leading up to the house and rang the doorbell.

'Love you so much. We will talk tomorrow as I am home now.' I said.

She knew what I had to endure at home and so knew better than to keep me on the phone any longer. 'Okay love you. See you tomorrow.' She rang off.

I popped my mobile in my pocket when suddenly the door flung open with force. Before I could even comprehend what was happening I was grabbed violently by the lapels and thrust into the house by a drunken and psychopathic Terry. I went hurtling in with such ferocity, I felt my teeth rattle in my head.

The next few minutes were hazy as blow after excruciating blow landed in my stomach and face. WHAM! SMACK! THUD! Dalj was right he was a killer and finally my number was up…

Chapter 3

Crunch time

Every crunching strike caused me to whimper like a puppy. I felt trickles streaming from several areas on my face and the taste of blood was patently swirling in my mouth. In-between the violent attack I could hear the ranting expletives and foul mouthed abuse that I had become accustomed to ringing around the walls of the small hallway that was now slowly becoming my tomb. Dalj was right about Terry, he had the look of a killer and right now I was about to appear as another notch on his victim list such was the bile laced savagery that I was confronted with. I fell to the floor for the third time, this time from the whipping and slashing from a belt. As I fell and before I was picked up again for another damaging onslaught I saw Myleene laying face down motionless through the gap in the living room door. Was she dead? I grimaced, I was soon about to join her on the pyre of doom. Then, all of a sudden – nothing, I daren't look up but my survival instinct implored me to see where the next fist was coming from. I braced myself lifting my face out of a pool of my own sick and vomit and glanced up squinty eyed. Terry was already half way up the stairs when he stopped and turned to look at me.

'Next time let me know when you decide to pop out around that ab jabs house. Oh and I heard about your trip to Mumbai. Yes, that's right your teacher phoned here first and told me everything. You are not going – you hear me?' His scowling words were the cherry on top of the maniacal violence that had been dished out by the brute.

It took me several minutes before I could muster up enough strength to slope off up to my room. As I limped in I saw a scene of utter carnage and devastation. My posters of actors were ripped to shreds and lying in a pile in the middle of the room. My acting certificates were defaced and many torn up, with all my trophies smashed to smithereens too. It was the work of the Devil, the work of Terry, the violent and supercilious animal. I had to escape before he finished off the job, my life had just become even more perilous…

Wednesday 8th July - I woke up the next day and could hear Myleene cackling like a witch downstairs. It seemed that the old hag had survived her drunken binge the night before and I now realised had been sprawled out from the crates of booze she had consumed. I heard Terry mention my name and then more cackling followed.

It was clear that the gutless worm was relaying details of the sickening and unprovoked attack on me last night, and Myleene was lapping up every rib shattering detail like the drunken ghoul she was. I then shuddered when I heard Terry whisper, 'The money will soon be ours, and then we can get him under foster care or something…he owes us big time the little parasite, blood sucker, leech…'

'Oi, that's out of order!' Myleene chipped in quickly.

Finally, she had come to her senses I thought hanging on to this tiny crumb of comfort and newly discovered ally, 'You forgot hanger on, sponger and freeloader, ha ha.' The uproarious and sinister shrilling that followed would not have looked out of place in a horror movie, except this was no movie but the guillotine swinging knife edge that my existence had boiled down to. I was in extremis and an upside down volatile dystopia.

I waited patiently for ages whilst playing a selection of Bhangra tracks in the background. Finally, I heard the front door shut as they both sloped off to get their weekly dole cheques. Today was my birthday. I was officially eighteen and I had arranged to visit my bank and sort out the paperwork to get my money as it would essentially fund my travel to India. Terry and Myleene did not have any idea when I was going to turn eighteen. The years of alcohol abuse had dulled their wits and senses so much that they were more concerned as to where their next can of lager was coming from. This was of no concern to me and I attended the bank and got the relevant access via cards and cheque books that I needed to my money. An account was set up so that I would be able to withdraw the money even whilst I was in India. After that, I met up with Dalj and Prity in Patel's Coffee Haven next door to Thames Valley Uni in Slough. We sat there and discussed my great escape.

'Why weren't you at Uni today and what happened to your lip?' Asked a concerned looking Prity.

'Oh I slipped over and cut my lip, clumsy or what hey? So I thought I would skip Uni otherwise I might have got strange looks from the others.' I scanned their reactions and they had fallen for my acting hook, line and sinker. I was getting good.

'Sam, did you get your money?' Dalj asked.

'Yeah thanks mate. I took out a couple of thousand today because I am serious about going you know.'

'What money?' Prity asked. She was well ensconced within my circle of trust so I told her about the money and she remained supportive.

'Do what you need to do with your goals like I said to you, but make sure you build a small memorial to your parents somewhere here with some of the money, otherwise you will not have their blessing in the future.' Prity's words made sense to me.

'I will do that love.' I said.

'Yeah good idea.' Dalj chipped in.

'So guys I have decided to go and want you both to go with me. What do you say?'

'How long you thinking?' asked Dalj.

'I don't know, maybe a couple of weeks.'

'Ahh, problem. What about the visas? Dalj was as sharp as a tack.

'I know someone who can sort any visas out fast track, so if you are serious about going then I say let's do this.' I turned to Prity and held her hand, 'Babes you sure you want to come too?'

'Yeah I think it will be a great laugh.' Prity reassured me.

Dalj suggested that we should go and see a pundit that he knew of just to get the blessing we needed for this remarkable opportunity. It was almost an indoctrinated family tradition that the Agarwal's upheld before any major event. It gave them the reassurance to forge ahead with the blessing from the God's.

It was also to find out if there were any precautions that we would need to take prior to the trip; such as throwing coconuts into water, tap dancing on nails in your bare feet, or something equally ridiculous.

Dalj was great when it came to looking out for me in situations like this. So, off we went in search of the best gun slinging pundit this side of town.

The first advert we stumbled across in the back of the weekly Asian paper was for the ostentatious Mr Varma Shah, a spiritual God. The advert stated that he had the skills to pay the bills. This virtuoso of the spirit world could while away your troubles with the deft flick of a coconut such was the write up accompanying his photo. His picture in the paper had already amused me and he looked as though he had been dragged through a hedge backwards such was the state of his frazzled hair. We sat in the front room of his house, a terraced brick built place in the heart of Southall. Mr Shah, the high priest of bollockso, the ancient art of pulling the wool over your eyes as he rifled your pockets sat there in his pyjamas and waistcoat. I mean what the hell was that about? I looked on painfully. This bloke looked as though he had just escaped a comic strip. I sensed there were cartoon illustrators scouring the earth looking for him, either that or the fashion police. He never looked at us for the entire time that Dalj and I sat there, but instead examined the rolled up piece of paper he held in his hand and made little notes on the paper with a pen. I looked closely and noticed that he had the property page open and was seemingly putting down the deposit on his next house as the two gullible dummies, namely us, sat before him.

'So I will need five hundred pounds to do a prayer for you. Then I will take this blessing to some water and you will receive good luck.' His demand was painful and ludicrous.

'Hold on a minute pal. Where do you buy your magic potions from, the bloody estate agents?'

I said sarcastically. The master of spin must have thought he had a pair of mugs trussed up like money trees sat cooped up in front of him, two smart as a door knob suckers to fleece for every last dime. The pundit almost fell off his seat and I could see the white's of his eyes when he realised the net closing in on him, his eyes remained wide with sucker punching shock. Suffice to say that our visit to this pundit was short lived, and I had to be physically restrained from tying him up with cheese wire in the boot of the car and dangling him over a bridge by his nose hairs. I felt insulted and wound up that this wormy vulture and toe sucking cretin preyed on the weak and vulnerable with the dollar signs spinning like an arcade machine in his eyes when he sniffed some business coming his way. Rituals - the only ritual he needed was a good old fashion poker straight up where the sun doesn't shine, that would have mended his duplicitous ways I thought angrily.

Later that evening I met up with Prity in the local pub – The Dog and Biscuit, in Burnham, near Slough.

I used this time to convey my concerns with what I had overheard in the morning when Terry and Myleene had been conspiring to get their grubby mitts on my money.

It was unfathomable to me that my dad's brother, the alcoholic butt head that he was could be so callous and calculating in his bid to siphon money from me in such a manner. I mean all he had to do was ask and I would have given him some money if that is what he really wanted. I guess some people have character whilst others in life are characters, and in his case he was the latter and not a pleasant one at that. Prity looked shocked at my revelations and tried to console me by placing her arms around me. It was a nice gesture and lifted my weary spirit somewhat. She truly was the holly to my ivy and her beauty and soft demure naturally demanded my obedience.

We stayed for a little bit longer and after a few drinks and more conversation, we got up to leave. We walked outside into the car park and held hands as we strolled leisurely up towards the exit.

WHAM! I felt a blow to my face and heard Prity screaming. I fell to the deck clutching the side of my face in agony. I quickly stumbled back to my feet and looked up to see an Asian guy pulling Prity by the hair and trying to kiss her as she fought him off bravely, screaming and shouting at him to leave her alone.

I charged over to him without any care for my safety and wrestled with him, finally releasing his lecherous grip from her. It was the opportune moment for me to reach down into my pants and feel that I had a pair. Suddenly we stood there facing one another. I recognised him. It was the barn brawling Anil, the guy from Singh's Drama School, and the self acclaimed Indian Tony Montana.

The violent and wayward hood who had snubbed the acting school to pursue a life of crime and dodging bullets. His reputation had preceded him and I knew he was capable of serving me up a Colombian neck tie, where your throat is slit and your tongue is pulled out from the gaping wound in your neck at the mere drop of a hat and without provocation.

'What the hell do you think you are doing Anil?' I asked disturbingly, my face still throbbing from his cheap shot punch and with the taste of the sidewalk still fresh on my mouth. He had turned into a violent street mugger I thought worryingly at the time.

'Thought you could get rid of me did you? I paid for your drama fees, kept you in acting and now you and that fucker Spiros get the break to go to India. You are not even Asian white boy! What the fuck is all that about?'

Anil looked like he had just been chewing on a plateful of wasps for dinner. His venomous scowl and aggressive manoeuvring was unnerving and he actually scared me. What did he mean by Spiros? He was an actor from the drama school who was generally disliked by all for many reasons.

'Look mate, I will pay you back the fees. Thanks and all that, but I never saw you to give you your money.'

'I never saw you, I never saw you.' Anil put on a girly voice as he mocked what I had said.

'I am not difficult to find you arse wipe.' Anil looked at Prity and smirked, 'She's alright ain't she? What you saying you hooker fancy a real man tonight or do you just pork dweebs? Hell I bet she ain't even opened her legs for you yet player, ha ha.'

Sweet mother of God - every fibre, every nerve in my body was straining to punch him but I relented and touched the side of my face where he had punched me and felt the pain shoot back up to my brain. This grounded me in an instant and I let him rant and rave hoping that he would slink off somewhere once he had had his tantrum.

'Listen boy, I am all out of favours. No more free drama fees, I want the dosh in your bank. I want two hundred big ones before you fuck off to India, and if I don't get it then...' Anil looked at Prity in a sickening manner and then back at me. 'I will ruin her so hard that you will end up killing yourself in utter shame. Capiche?'

I looked on with pure hatred, as did Prity.

'Just remember the saying that one man's death is another's bread. It makes no difference to me if you live or you die, I have a habit to feed, people that I need to keep on my side and I just want a cash injection – fast!'

With that, he turned and slipped away into the shadows of the night. I walked over to Prity and tried to hug her but she looked revolted and pulled away as a reflex action before calming down and settling into my arms.

She started to cry, sob uncontrollably,' You must tell someone about this. He can't get away with it, he just can't. I'll give him the money, plea...'

'No stop babes. Look, I have a plan. We will go to India and get away from this idiot. He will never find us and then I will sort it when I get back.

'Sam. Listen to me. This guy has convictions for stabbing people, I have heard he is dangerous and hangs around with a big gang in Slough. These dudes are reckless animals and I am scared, I really am.' She hugged me so tight I thought that she was trying to pump the alcohol out of my system. So the guy could eat my liver off a plate, what was there to worry about, I mused?

'Ssshhh, okay calm down, it will be okay.' The desperation hung from my lips and I secretly knew it wouldn't be as my sphincter twitched like it was going out of fashion, but my words were soothing enough to pour the necessary oil on this evening's troubled waters. I escorted her home and that night I slept with one eye open. I needed to chat with dad and get his advice. There were now so many twisted forks in the road I was one confused bunny. I needed guidance, a helping hand and a torch light to emancipate me from this ever burgeoning quagmire that my life was slowly becoming. The worse part of the night was the Freudian slip that Anil had made about Spiros being invited on the trip as well. That was seriously not funny and I knew he was the quintessential psycho. He was one twitch away from a lunatic asylum and even Pinto was a steadfast normal functioning saint in his company. My heart felt heavy and bruised. What drama would tomorrow offer me up? I was afraid, very afraid...

Chapter 4

Human faeces detector

Thursday 9th July - Today I booked up the tickets, sorted the visas, and got the necessary injections that I needed and instructed Dalj and Prity to do the same. All this was managed around University classes.

We were due to fly out on Sunday and we were all very excited. I was now beginning to feel the love and it was great to look forward to a life changing trip and it was what I needed to take the thorn out of my paw after some of the recent exploits I had been dragged into. It was a time for a clean sweep with an iron broom and my bones craved the opportunity with unbridled zeal.

After our Economics class I took Prity to one side and asked if she was okay after the traumatic evening that we had. In the short time that I had got to know her I knew she was a bit of a worrier. She was a kind of heart on the sleeve girlfriend and her moods were very much dictated by what was bubbling away in her head. She reassured me and we were soon joined by Dalj, and we filled him in with the drama. He did not look amused and shared his concerns with us. The conversation ebbed and flowed and we all talked fervently about the forthcoming trip to India. I could hardly believe that we were all actually going out together.

For the first time in eons, my heart was singing. I had always loved everything about the Indian culture, from the food, the funky Bhangra and down to the good hearted nature of the people. Added to this wonderful mix was having my beautiful Indian princess by my side along with my close Punjabi friend in Dalj, these factors really were the cherries on top.

'So this is it guys. We are really getting away from it all.' I said to both of them as they stared at me in nervous anticipation.

'Have you spoken to Visperal again? You know about what is going to happen on the trip?' asked Dalj.

'Oh it is simple, we go to the airport meet a guy called Baldip, who is then assigned to take us around the Bollywood film studios and introduce us to anyone who is a someone. I get to audition a few times, we have good food, lovely conversation and above all network with the stars and directors, because that is how you get yourself known in the industry.'

Dalj crackled into life and said,' I have heard the industry is hard to break into. They say that it is run and largely influenced by the major families - The Bacchan's, the Kapoor's, the Oberoi's, the Khanna's, the Khan's, the Dutt's, the Anand's…'

'The Babbar's and the Devgan's,' chipped in Prity.

'Yeah I know, but you have to start somewhere and at the moment I am holding the Willy Wonka golden ticket and to be frank with you I am getting the hell out of Nam.' I responded.

'Nam?' asked Prity curiously.

'Oh that is what I call the area between my front gate and the back of the house. It is a fricking war zone and definitely not for the faint hearted I tell you.'

The pair of them laughed, but without conviction.

'What are the plans?' asked Dalj.

'We fly out on Sunday so I will have to keep under the radar until that time. I will be off the phone, so only call me if it is mega urgent, just in-case Bonnie and Clyde are eaves dropping on my conversations, okay?

I spoke with a hint of apprehension in my voice. I was so used to things going wrong in my life that in my mind nothing was guaranteed, not until I strapped myself into the seat in the plane and took off. I knew that something or someone was itching to piss on my fireworks.

'Oh and don't mention it to anyone, or else my goose is well and truly cooked at home.' I sought their assurance.

'Ahh, I may have accidentally let slip mate.' Dalj mouthed the words that I dreaded and exemplifying perfectly the fact that he really did possess the I.Q. of a raisin.

I looked at him momentarily stunned, 'What do you mean. Have you told Terry? My face was beginning to contort from sheer disappointment. I knew Dalj was loquacious by nature and thus should have seen this coming. Maybe he was trying to scupper my chances of success, maybe he wanted to foil my trip as he was jealous. I remained silent and waited eagerly for his response.

'I let slip to my mum and dad…that you were going…I am sorry.' He looked upset for some reason, but this was short lived as I puffed out my cheeks. The release of endorphins raced around my veins. 'Is that all? You told your parents.' I was so happy.

'Yeah that is all Sam,' he assured me.

'And what about Terry? I take it he has no idea about when I am getting away?' I asked him.

'I have no idea as I have not spoken to him.' Dalj had saved the day.

'What did your mum and dad say when you told them? Do they think I am crazy just upping and going? I asked.

'Nah trust me they are well excited for you. Dad even said that he wished he could go out there with you and support you, especially as you don't know the country and industry at all. He mentioned that it could be quite cut throat if you were not connected.'

'Really, that is cool.' I said. It was reassuring to know that I had such stalwart support from his parents, especially considering they knew the pains that I had been enduring on my young shoulders for such a long time.

'Hey, mum was even talking about needing a trip, so you never know, they may just turn up Sam. They do crazy stuff like that and I wouldn't put it past them.' Dalj laughed.

'Look put all that to one side honey. You just need to get out there and escape this quagmire that your life has become. Your parents' would want you to pursue your dreams, so forget all the hang ups and go and do it for Gods' sake. You have a bank full of money and now it is your time to see how the chips fall for you. This could be the making of you, you never know. You will never find out unless you venture out there and see if you get your break in the industry.' Prity spoke a lot of sense and her words edified me in an instant.

'Just think you can get away from pricks like Terry, gold diggers like Myleene, oh and not to mention what's his face…Anil last night with his bone idle threats about this that and the other. Think about it, what can he do if you are over in India? Hey, is he going to come out there and visit you? I don't think so!'

She was on the money with her assessment of the situation and had conveyed her feelings exceptionally well.

'Nah, you are right. At least I will be able to get away from all that unnecessary tension and the vexations in my life for a while. Great, I am looking forward to it even more now.' I leaned over and kissed her on the lips. They tasted succulent, and not only that they god damn tasted of cherries. She kissed me back and then pulled away suddenly realising that we had company, as Dalj sat there in true voyeuristic fashion with his binoculars, trench coat and green finger nails fiddling with the belt on his trousers.

'Oh you two get a room,' he murmured.

We laughed hard and nestled back into our seats as we chatted for a few moments more before we said our goodbyes for the day and headed off to our respective homes.

Now I always had a dreaded feeling whenever I walked up the driveway to uncle Terry's house. The abuse and beatings were only an open door away. I felt this nauseating feeling as I opened the front door with the key.

I walked in, sensing something was wrong. I was like an animal smelling the impending danger across the threshold of the hallway. The pendulum of doom felt like it was swinging my way as I took those tentative steps through the living room door.

'Come here mate, grab a seat,' motioned a red faced and suitably sozzled Terry sitting on the chair opposite me with a wooden coffee table acting as a barrier between us.

Oh, here we go again I mused painfully. I sat down dejectedly. I figured by now that the beatings were just a part of growing up as I looked on in disappointed anticipation.

'Where is the money your folks left you in their will? Is it in your bank account?' His voice carried a sinister malevolence and caution.

He sat on the sofa opposite and studied me carefully for a reaction. I was painfully aware that one Freudian slip, one spoonerism or other faux pas would result in my guts being spilled out across the carpet - that was for sure. I glanced over nervously at the belt resting on the mantelpiece. I could see that it still housed sickening remnants of my blood splattering from erstwhile beatings that he had meted out to me. I remained silent. For some reason my mouth stayed glued shut. I went to answer but I froze. This only exacerbated the situation and Terry repeated. 'I am not in the habit of asking the same question more than once, where is the money?' He shuffled up from the sofa and sat perched on the edge. I inadvertently sucked in the cheap and stale booze from his mouth as it wafted over in my direction. It made me want to retch, but I refrained somehow.

He had me on the polygraph, the human lie detector and I was not escaping unchecked. The lie detector is used for recording several physiological responses including blood pressure, your pulse, respiration, body temperature, and breathing rhythm, all measured whilst you are asked a series of questions.

Terry the wily fox that he was scrutinised me like the quintessential polygraph - probing and analysing everything I said as he began to fire a myriad of questions relating to the money at me. This bombardment continued as he tested (like a polygraph does) the physiological changes in my nervous system. I suppose it could have been worse as I was vaguely aware of some other lie detector type tests that were carried out around the world according to the history books, including one such practice in Africa whereby people suspected of a crime were asked to pass a bird's egg to one another. If a person broke the egg they would be considered guilty, based on the idea that their nervousness was to blame. I was just thinking of the mess there would have been on my hands and the carpet due to the amount of eggs that I would have been smashing through my jangled nerves, and my reluctance to say anything about my financial situation to the monster sitting in front and gawking at me like I was a parasite.

I also recalled that in ancient China, suspects were made to hold a handful of rice in their mouths during a prosecutor's speech as it was suspected that salivation was believed to cease at times of emotional anxiety. The person was considered guilty if by the end of that speech the rice was dry. I could already feel my throat and tongue were like sandpaper and akin to the most baron part of the Sahara Desert.

'When are you going to wake up and realise that there is no fucking Yellow Brick Road? There isn't no god damn OZ and there is no chance of you making it in Pakiwood or whatever it is called. You hear that sound? Listen carefully.'

His eyes scanned the room and we both tuned into a hollow tapping sound that could be heard. Hear it? The tapping continued as he brought his hand up from underneath the coffee table where he had been tapping it and then repeated it on the top of the table. Now that is the sound of reality knocking and saying get your fucked up head out of the sand and give up this stupid pipe dream of yours or I will...oh FUCK IT!' Terry had said enough, or not as the case was here and stood up sharply and with volcanic rage, his grasping hand yanking the belt from its resting place on the mantelpiece. I heard the bell sounding for round one and quickly curled up into a ball, covering up the essential areas such as the crown jewels and face. The rest of me was used to and conditioned to receiving bone crushing blows over the years.

So, there it was, the angels on my shoulder were on their knees praying for leniency but the die was already cast. WHACK! CRASH! WHIP! SMACK! – it was like a scene out of a Batman movie. The blows rained down on me with furious intention and unnerving accuracy. CRUNCH! WALLOP! – The torturous nightmare continued, interspersed with excited expletives. I had already switched my mind off and knew I just had to survive in one piece. I had to survive a little while longer and I knew I would be emancipated from this world of hurt. I had often thought about fighting back, of growing a pair and turning the tables. The reality however was different to my fantasised notions of a fight back. I knew that my skinny frame, one that was devoid of any tangible and credible muscles would not stand much chance against a seasoned bruiser like Terry. It was just not happening, so as per usual I lay there like an ever bruising possum until after a few more minutes of whacking he stopped and walked out slamming the front door behind him. I opened my eyes, they were blurry and everything looked foggy and white. Maybe that was it – I was in heaven. This is what it looked like, great. I did not pass Go and I did not collect two hundred pounds but instead I had just jumped on a no frills airline straight to my maker. I wallowed in these surreal thoughts for a moment or two, even casting aside the trickles of blood I could suddenly sense seeping down my forehead from one or two hits that had bounced off my skull.

Suddenly my eyes opened wide and glared at the entrance to the kitchen. I could see Medusa - a.k.a, Myleene sauntering in to the scene of my near demise. What had she been doing in the kitchen, measuring up my coffin, talking to the undertaker? I was in pain and I was confused. I looked up for mercy with the widest and most pleading eyes I could muster up. I mean any wider and my eyeballs would have fallen out of their sockets. She walked up close and personal just so she could sniff up the fresh blood, surely, she did not want to finish me off I grimaced? My bones simply did not have any resistance left in them. I prepared myself for round two and the finishing blows.

'I saw everything and to be honest I am surprised he didn't kill you,' she added in a bid to settle my frayed nerves.

Thanks for that you ditzy old bat, just what I needed to hear after I was almost beaten to within one inch of my miserable life.

'If I were you I would withdraw the money and just give it to him or I reckon he will get carried away when he starts drinking again.' She threw the statement and chilling log on to my fire and sat back waiting for a reaction as she skulked nearby.

Ah, I get it, the old good cop, bad cop routine was being played a treat on me.

'I was not impressed. 'Can I go to my room?' I asked nervously and patently refusing to answer anymore questions. I had taken enough hurt, abuse and above all humiliation for one day to let this sadistic shit bag of an auntie patronise me one iota longer.

'Do what you want, but I would think about going to the bank in the morning mate,' she hiccupped, burping what I could only suggest was vodka from her venomous cake hole.

With that, I slinked off to the sanctum of my bedroom, locked the door and cried myself to sleep in my pillow, sobbing until the dams were well and truly dry. I had to escape this hell hole and Bollywood seemed like my only respite from this peril, my last ditch hope…I prayed to God…

Chapter 5

Hasta luego amigo

Sunday 12th July - We gathered at Heathrow airport in what Dalj said to me was typical Indian style, with overly packed suitcases and Dalj's clothes reeking of haldi (a strange pungent Asian aroma used as a paste for cooking). The smell wafted chokingly through the land side lounge as Dalj continued busting out Punjabi tracks on speaker from his mobile unaware of the carnage he was leaving in his wake.

'Mate, that is an interesting after shave you have on,' I said sarcastically.

Prity smiled knowingly as we checked in our suitcases and made our way through to airside.

Just as we were about to walk through the control gate the silence was earth shatteringly destroyed.

'Oi, kidda paajee,' a voice boomed across from the other side of the airport. I looked up as did the other hundred or so passengers.

There strolling through majestically were Dalj's dad, his mum and a straggling Pinto, her tiny feet shuffling as quick as they could so as to keep up with them. I looked at Prity who had a quizzical look on her face and then at Dalj. He was smiling and had the kind of Beadles about stroke Jim'll Fix It look about him. I was not sure what was coming but as they drew closer to me my sphincter began to twitch like a jack hammer.

'You didn't think we would let you guys go to India all on your own did you?' Karpal said.

'Huh!' My retort shamefully inadequate and nonsensical in the circumstances.

'No, these kids are sensible dear, we just thought you could do with some company, that's all.' Saraswati the voice of reason piped up.

'What...are you coming to India with us?' asked Prity. Her voice carried an air of disappointment.

'No she said she wanted to go and see her home land.' Saraswati's interjection was clinical and brought some transparency to the spiralling situation.

'That is so retarded that's what that is,' whispered Prity by my side, clearly seething from this unwelcome intrusion on our trip.

I must admit the invitation was as inspiring as a warty nipple and I was internally spitting feathers but kept the fake smile plastered on my face and acted sublimely.

'Yeah mate, hope you don't mind but I told mum and dad about the trip before and they insisted that grandma came so that she can get some fresh air in India.' Dalj said openly.

'Pinto insisted that she wanted to come along too. How could I have stopped her?' Dalj added.

I looked at her goofy face, she was insatiable and with those sad puppy eyes and white moustache hairs hanging over her upper lip it was a done deal.

'Err..cheers mate, that's cool.' What else could I have said without witnessing Pinto keeling over with a heart attack if I had refused to let her travel with us. At the end of the day, I was certain that she would not be a hindrance on this trip and I would keep her in the confines of the hotel complex so that she did not get up to any mischief. Prity's face still resembled a bulldog chewing several wasps and she hastily made her way through the controls after saying her goodbyes to Dalj's mum and dad. Dalj hugged them and then followed Prity. Pinto hooked her hand on to the back of my belt almost pulling my combats down as I ushered her through the control. I waved goodbye to the stitch up merchants, Dalj's mum and dad and we made our way airside.

Pinto kept looking at me throughout this short walk with a mushy smile plastered across her face, bless her, she was harmless. The worse case scenario I secretly hoped was that the Mumbai sunshine would activate some of her dormant grey cells and give her some sensibility about her surroundings. I did not hold up much hope, but it was worth a try and failing that I would incarcerate her in the hotel room, give her a bowl of soup, some stale bread and stick her in front of the fan so she could entertain herself by watching it whirr. At least that would keep the loopy old bat off my case while I fulfilled my dream.

We headed off to our gate. I had been informed that Spiros would be meeting us at the airport and cringingly awaited the magical moment when he made his appearance. We settled into the seats by our gate and bided our time with conversational pleasantries whilst waiting the half an hour or so before our flight departed.

The attendant called for passengers to start embarking the plane and all of a sudden there was a mad dash for the gate. I looked around and felt a wave of relief sweeping though my body. There was absolutely no sign of Spiros. Maybe he had forgotten about the trip, it was not as though I was going to phone him to remind him to pack his toothbrush or anything. Prity escorted Pinto on to the plane and I slowly followed Dalj in the queue. Pinto insisted on sitting next to me and excitedly said that she wanted the window seat. She asked me to get some vaseline for her chapped and withering lips from her hand luggage whilst she made herself comfortable.

Prity sat next to me on the other side and Dalj sat across us in the aisle. I stood up and opened the overhead locker to rummage around in Pinto's bag. Several seconds later, I found the vaseline hidden intricately amongst her dozen or so white chunnis (head scarves), white suits and a moisty jar for her dentures. I guess she digged the colour white. I started to bring it out whilst turning triumphantly towards Pinto like a conquering hero. Suddenly, my wrist was grabbed hard with vice like intent and precision.

This jolted me, the vaseline dropping out of my hand and back into the bag. I turned quickly and looked into the eyes of Lucifer himself. It was Spiros, the venomous cretin with his black wavy hair hanging off his square head, the tips resting on his shoulders. He was a brooding beast of a guy with a Desperate Dan chin that had patently been no stranger to solvent abuse over the years. He shifted his stocky Popeye type frame over to us with all the smugness of an over confident buffoon. At five feet ten inches he wasn't particularly imposing in the height stakes but he more than made up for it with his rippling muscles bulging out from his jean jacket, I mean I could actually see his six pack through his clothing. More to the point, what was he doing wearing a jean jacket? Those babies were surely buried under the dust of history I sniggered to myself.

He looked me up and down in disgust whilst still controlling my wrist. I tried to free my arm but my efforts were in vain. He was strong and fierce. I stood no chance and took my medicine like a big boy.

'You had better lie down when it comes to the auditions or you will be coming back from India alright…in a box!' He scowled as he spoke, his mouth foaming. I quickly concluded in-between wetting my pants that he was either very angry or had just contracted rabies. I gulped hard, cartoon style.

Spiros released my hand by throwing it back into my body and sniffed hard before returning to his seat at the front of the plane. The stake had just been driven through any glimmer of support I thought I would be getting from my acting companion and I realised then that all bets were off for any kind of blossoming friendship too.

I looked down at Prity. She was helping Pinto with her seatbelt and had not seen what had happened. Similarly, Dalj was too busy window licking to notice the near death experience and I suddenly felt so alone and so pressured. Why did this always happen to me?

I slinked back into my seat, completely beaten up and rattled by the encounter. This trip had doom written all over it. Spiros had threatened me to take a fall during the auditions thus ensuring he got the part and eliminating me from the process. This was evil, sick and underhand, but what could I have done, he was a bruising whirlwind of a bully and I was painfully aware that even on an off day he had the minerals to mop the floor up with me with just the hairs in his nostrils.

The journey took us around eight hours and throughout that time there were several near death experiences whereby Pinto in her fragile state of mind would suddenly stand up on her seat and start to scream that an infestation of mice had snuck on to the plane. It was another example of her inherent phobia with the small furry rodents. I would struggle to yank her back down and wrestle her back into her seat. In another barmy moment she started to hurl peanuts across the plane in an almost child like manner. I would give her stern warnings and she would stop, but then continue a few minutes later, resulting in me confiscating the bag of Hajmola nuts that she had smuggled on to the plane. Pinto was a card and really should have had cameras following her around, great entertainment value sometimes and hair pulling agony at other times.

She eventually calmed down and was later in her element reading the lines on everyone's hands, called the 'haathon ki lahkerein – meaning the lines of fate. She done me, the people sat in the seats in front and even the air hostesses, telling them of what great adventures they would see in their life, of some tragedy, but fun times nevertheless. It was basically the bleeding obvious and kept her amused for a good few hours before she rested her weary head back on the head rest and snored herself to the land of nod.

My mind was preoccupied with other thoughts and my dream was fizzling out before it had even started. I had the raving lunatic Pinto by my side, the looming threat of Spiros so near, the sinister thought of Anil nestled firmly in the back of my mind but tangibly threatening when I returned to the UK – successful or not, and not to forget Terry and Myleene, the double act baying for my blood upon my return. It did not get any worse I thought as I closed my eyes for some much needed shut eye. My only hope was for a successful break in Mumbai, India, the place where dreams could possibly come true.

We had reached our destination safe and sound and headed off like a herd of cattle through the security procedures at the airport.

Here we were in India, the land of spirituality, philosophy and birth place to some religions that are not even in existence today.

After much procrastination and kerfuffle, we walked into the dizzy midday sunshine of Mumbai, formerly known as Bombay in the state of Maharashtra. There were several theories why the name had been changed. Some have said that Bombay was the corrupted version of Mumbai used by the British during the colonial rule, others believed it related to the theory that the Portuguese referred to is as 'Bombaim' when they arrived in the sixteenth century, and then others saying that it was named after the Hindu God - Mumbadevi.

Either way the name was changed in the nineties and funny enough was always referred to as Mumbai by the inhabitants long before anyway, it was only the West who called it Bombay. I scanned my surroundings and saw reams and reams of rickshaws, taxi's and people milling around, it was truly mesmerising. I had never witnessed anything like his before. It was surreal. There were thousands of people. I mean it was awe inspiring. I had been told that an agent called Baldip had been arranged to meet us at the airport, but I took one look and I knew that I would have more chance of finding the smallest needle in the largest hay stack then locate tracing an agent called Baldip.

I asked Dalj to keep an eye on Pinto as I paced up and down the concourse searching in vain for Baldip.

'Mr Miers?'

I turned on a six pence. There stood in front of me was a small chap, wearing round glasses, with a Brylcream hairstyle swept over to one side. He spoke in a posh voice.

'You must be Baldip,' I said quite astonished that he had honed in on us so swiftly.

'Yes, I am Baldip. Please ask your friends to join me.' He pointed to a minibus across the street.

'How did you find us so qui…?'

'I have photo's you see, come come, we must go.' He ushered me forwards with him.

I motioned for the others to follow me and soon we were getting into the minibus. Baldip got in to drive and my heart sank as I saw the passenger sitting next to him was none other than Spiros. He simply exchanged an evil look with me. Spiros introduced himself to Dalj, Prity and Pinto and everything seemed pleasant from their perspective. If only they knew the murky undertone that was pervading throughout the minibus.

Within seconds, we had set off on the journey to our hotel. Baldip had arranged to put us up in the Hotel Dell Ebelee. He assured us that it was a mere fifteen minutes stone throw away from the mammoth Bollywood film studios - now that was an impressive throw I thought. My heart was racing from the excitement of it all. I had made it thus far. A lifelong dream was being played out before my very eyes. The fact that I was in the same city in the palace of dreams was so enriching. I squeezed Prity's hand hard as the minibus shuttled its way treacherously through the traffic. I sprouted wings several times on that journey from near misses with gigantic lorries and trucks. How we ended up parked outside the hotel in the fifteen minute journey was a surprise in itself.

We entered the wonderful hotel's reception with its veneered furniture, comfortable armchairs nestled in the corner and the centrepiece a cascading water fountain shimmering away with delectable brilliance.

It was a welcome release from the throbbing, suffocating realties of the sweltering and humid city with its thirteen million folk eking out their next tuppance.

Baldip assisted us in checking in to our rooms. Spiros got a room to himself. Dalj and Pinto shared a room and Prity and I got a room for us. Baldip said that he lived quite far away from the hotel and said that he would be here every morning without quibble to rouse us for the day ahead. We all appreciated the gesture.

That evening we all shared a few drinks in the hotel bar. Baldip refrained as he had a pressing engagement and said that he would join us in the morning.

Spiros was unbelievably friendly to me whilst in the company of the others. This was disconcerting and I was not sure how to play this. He even offered to buy me a drink such was his generosity that evening. He was already on course for a Bollywood Oscar I thought.

One by one everyone slowly headed up to their rooms. I sat there and took out my wallet and a picture from within. The tears started to stream down my cheeks. What was all this about? I sobbed.

I looked down at happier days, mum and dad were sat on the verdant grass of my local park with me nestled securely in dad's arms as a young five year old. I loved them so much and they reciprocated by giving me the best childhood I could have ever have hoped for. The knot in my stomach tightened and my throat began to ache as the tears gushed downwards soaking my tee shirt without remorse. I shook my head and looked out of the window into the emptiness of the night. The deep heart-felt bruising in my heart was a pain that you can only suffer and realise when you have truly lost someone close to you, someone who means the world to you. This pain was always there locked away and buried deep in the bowels of my heart, It was at poignant times like these that I unlocked the chamber of hurt and allowed my emotions to run amok with unbridled freedom, just to feel the crushing reality of esoteric pain that destroyed my personality that fateful day. I wiped my eyes with a napkin and stroked my parents' faces on the photo. I would do this for them I reassured myself. I would make it in Bollywood. I took one last swig of my Bacardi and coke and made my way up to my room. I needed to rest, or jet lag would be responsible for below par performances from me. I also needed time to consider what Spiros had threatened me with in the plane. What consequences awaited me if I were to ignore the threatening words of Spiros? The knot in my stomach remained there as I cuddled up next to my beautiful girlfriend that night and drifted off into the abyss, uncertain as to the depth of danger that lurked surreptitiously nearby. How real was the threat? I was just about to find out…

Chapter 6

Viva la India

I woke up the next morning to the aromatic smell of cow dung wafting in through the open window of our hotel room. Prity wrapped her silky legs around mine as she puckered up to kiss me, her perfume from last night still lingering tantalisingly from her soft body. She bought her lips closer to mine, soft, sexy and so kissable had it not been for the sewer type smell seeping from her mouth such was the toe curling stench of morning breath that threatened to eviscerate me where I lay.

Suddenly and thankfully, our attention was drawn to a knocking sound on the door to our room. I jumped out of the bed with Superman type reflexes and headed off to the door. I had been saved by the bell and the thought of slurpy French kisses in the morning where we would be exchanging saliva laced halitosis was not my cup of Indian chai. I don't think Prity noticed as she quickly headed off to the en suite bathroom to patch herself up for the day ahead.

I opened the door and let a fresh faced Baldip into my lair.

'Good morning to you sir,' he said as he skipped in full of unbridled zest.

'Yeah, how you doing? Excuse the mess. Come in.'

Baldip walked towards the window and gazed out at the sights. He must have been immune to the smell of cow dung as he did not flinch for a second whilst he heartily sucked up some air.

'Ahh, what a glorious day we have for you Sam. How is your stay so far?' He continued staring out of the window.

I started to get dressed, 'It is different to what I am used to but I like it. It is an experience I suppose.'

Baldip then walked towards me and said, 'I am going to show you around some of the local sights today and it will get you used to the people, the weather and more importantly the food. We don't want you getting Delhi belly now do we?' He chuckled to himself and headed to the door.

'We will all be waiting in the lobby, come down when you are ready.' Baldip left and at that moment Prity came out of the toilet, her make up applied and I must say she looked like an Indian princess and good enough to eat. I stood there for a moment salivating like a dog whilst she put her clothes on. Once we were both ready we met up with Baldip and the others, including a trendy looking Spiros with his sunglasses draped on top of his head, his shirt open to the third button and grisly chest air hanging over the lapels like a wild forest. With hair like that he would have been the ideal candidate for an audition as the Wolf man I thought childishly as we sat in Badlip's minibus for the tour of Mumbai's sights.

'So tomorrow is the big day is it?' Spiros asked Baldip.

'Yes tomorrow I will introduce you to Jaspal Verma. He is one of the most influential directors in Bollywood and he is the one who is holding the auditions for his latest film.' Baldip retorted.

'Confident are you?' Spiros glared at me, teasing and trying to obviously provoke me into a response.

I looked back at him and composed my reply, 'Yeah it will be interesting to see what Mr Verma is looking for.' Prity squeezed my hand out of eye shot of Spiros who once again had sat in the passengers seat next to Baldip who was driving. I shifted my eyes to Prity and she smiled back knowingly.

She was my biggest supporter and the fact that she was flying the flag beside me on this trip meant the world to me. With her masquerading with me, I knew it would be enough to fend off the unwarranted attention and threats from imbeciles such as Spiros et al. These thoughts calmed my ever fraying nerves as Baldip tackled the traffic in the bustling city. I have never been so scared in all my life. It was like being in a three dimensional movie with cars, trucks and rickshaws whizzing inches away from us, not to mention instant death at every conceivable angle. The constant tooting of horns and knife edged misses almost making me soil my pants more times than I care to remember.

The ride from our hotel was enough to make me suddenly think of the UK's Highway Code as my new found Bible and most revered book EVER! I could not fathom how there were not pile ups and major accidents at every junction. It seemed the larger the vehicle and the louder the horn dictated the right of way in this comic book every day scenario. Elsewhere you would have Mr Singh, his rickshaw laden to the hilt with suitcases, bags and other loads, pedalling for all his three rupees worth almost under the wheels of a fucking monster juggernaut with wheels bigger than the rickshaw itself and without him flinching or skipping a heartbeat. It was eye rubbing stuff and I pressed myself into the back of the seat praying that I did not suddenly hear the crunching and splattering of a rickshaw rider like Mr Singh under the wheels of the minibus. I looked over at Dalj and he had a face like he had lost one hundred rupees and found one rupee. He gripped the driver's headrest, his knuckles turning white and matching the colour of his face. Pinto looked like she was at Alton Towers and seemed to be exaggerating every turn and twist from the minibus by moving violently to one side then the other. Her antics whiled away the drive for the zany old bat.

We passed breath taking sights such as the Gateway to India, the landmark where King George V landed in India. It was the same arch that the most revered of saints, Gandhi, had passed though when he had returned from South Africa and was built by the people of Mumbai as a mark of respect. It shimmered so aesthetically and looked simply electrifying.

We also drove past the Chor Bazaar (translated 'the thieves market') with its teeming and mouth watering array of antiques. It was a place for those with deep pockets and purgatory and was truly a sight to behold. Baldip was the perfect tourist guide driving us around and allowing us to acclimatise ourselves with our new home for the next few days or so.

The streets were packed with people and in amongst them were a swathe of beggars hobbling around in dishevelled clothing, some carrying sickening injuries, others looking they had been maimed to bolster up their begging revenue. The beggars were dancing with the traffic, risking life and limb, slinking in and out of the shadows of the sun rays beating down on their bony shoulders.

Baldip explained that begging is often an organised industry with the really poor ones diced up into gangs by the beggar overlords and conversely the slightly wealthier beggars actually owning houses and rickshaws when they were not begging. The beggar chiefs took a daily commission from the beggars and often the children were kidnapped, drugged, beaten, and maimed to fetch a higher 'catch' when they trawled the streets. Women tourist were the preferred choice of victim/target as they would consistently buckle at the knees when they were exposed to the beggar's puppy eyes and wet noses, and often their arm or other limb ripped out of their sockets complete with severed veins flapping against the side of their body. The beggars knew that the women would take pity on them and cough up their tourist money like walking ATM machines.

This epitomised life in the twelve miles long Island of Mumbai where sixty per cent of the population actually stemmed from the slums, with that figure equating to some seven million people. In fact, many people in India actually referred to the city as 'Slumbay or Slumbai,' in an impudent swipe at the residents and alarming urban growth rate of the slums.

The population of India had increased dramatically since the partition in India in nineteen forty seven, and as a result the only affordable way to survive was in an over crowded shack in one of the slums. This was where poor water; inadequate drainage; weak infrastructure; pollution and infant mortality were the most alluring features that you had to look forward to on a daily basis, not to mention having a couple of rats as foot cushions every night as you stared up to the stars through the holes in your ceiling.

I was shocked by what I was witnessing and had to pinch myself several times during the tour, I had read about it and heard about it, but this was surreal.

We then saw the beautiful white Haji Ali Mosque that had been built to honour the Muslim saint Haji Ali, where he was subsequently buried. It was an unforgettable sight and one caressing the skyline like the most beautiful silhouette. I dabbed my chin as a dribble of saliva trickled out clearly demonstrating my awe and captivation of seeing this monument of magnificence.

Next up was Chowpatty Beach and its Ferris wheel whirring on the sands in front of us. There were thousands upon thousands of people prancing around and enjoying themselves under the powerful rays of the sun. It was such innocence, which truly immersed me in this once in a lifetime trip. There were no bottles of sun factor cream to be seen, no inconsequential twittering, just normal people spending carefree and quality times with their families. That summed up life for me, just being able to go to the beach and chill out with your loved ones and forget the strains and stresses that we all carry on our shoulders on a daily basis each and every day of our lives in the UK. This was nirvana right here and I loved every rupee gripping second that we spent gawking at the spread of happy punters by the beach.

Baldip then drove us past the remarkable two storey building where Mahatma Gandhi once lived. The place had been turned into a museum and apparently told the story of the struggles that Gandhi had endured seeking peace for India. I had now secured some string around my chin and around my head to stop my jaw crashing to the floor yet again. The place was visually stunning and the glow that this whistle stop tour had given me lasted for a few hours afterwards, kind of like the rush you get when you get off a white knuckle rollercoaster at a theme park.

He finally drove us past a plethora of Hindu temples and told us that Hinduism, a colourful religion with many God's and Goddesses, was the most dominant religion in India with up to eighty per cent of people being Hindu and that the religion had been developed around five thousand years ago. He mentioned that Islam was second with twelve per cent, and others such as Sikhism were two per cent, Christianity at three per cent and so forth. He then crucially explained the history behind India's great religions, with Hinduism, Buddhism and Jainism referred to as the creators of Indian philosophy. He explained how the word Hindu was originally a geographical description and Sanskrit for the word Sindhu, and referred to a person from the land of Sindhu. He said that according to Hindu's they believed that three Lords ruled the world, Brahma – the creator, Vishnu – the preserver and Shiva – the destroyer. This was all fascinating for me especially as I had been born into Christianity.

Moments later and not a moment too soon we emerged from the traffic pandemonium that was found by driving in any Indian city and found ourselves parking up in a local curry house, Samosa Hut.

We alighted the vehicle and took our places at an outdoor table for a spot of alfresco culinary delights.

The menus were brought to us by the waiter and we ordered some tasty food and beverages. There were no complaints as every one of us devoured the treats like the true gastronomes we were. I must have resembled the local escapee from the mental asylum due to my continual swishing and swiping away of the hordes of demonic flies that had decided to descend upon us that very day. I was convinced unquestionably that they were working in squadrons and platoons. I was being pincer struck on either side, with the bastard foot soldiers landing and then ducking and rolling their way to the morsels on our plates before flying off like the winged crusaders they were, with the loot firmly ensconced in their grubby little mitts. This was becoming so irritating and it meant that I could not truly kick back and enjoy the food.

'Don't worry, you will get used to it,' laughed Baldip as he slurped the spoonful of Chicken Dhansk into his mouth with a barbaric fly looking up at him whilst perched on his nose.

After several minutes of swishing and head ducking, I was becoming crazy and my swiping and swatting with the napkins was becoming more and more aggressive. It seemed that everyone else was used to the invasion of crazed flies but me and despite Prity's reassuring words to sit down I continued my Norman Bates type behaviour even picking up the menu and trying to splat one of the beasts as he sat on the table feasting on a piece of naan bread. SPLAT!

He was far too wily for an inexperienced greenhorn like me and moved swiftly to one side and then the other as several more splats missed him. He danced and moved like a gymnast avoiding the crushing venom of the demon fly splatter that I wielded like a gladiator in my hand. The Muhammad Ali of flies was a skilled practitioner and had outfoxed me in front of my colleagues. He smirked one last time and went to fly off to his haven, satisfied that his work had been executed to perfection.

WHAM! I swiped the menu down with all the strength that I could muster and caught the little bastard mid flight, his tiny yelp echoing in the open aired veranda. His bloody body clung to the menu as I followed through straight into the face of Spiros who was sat opposite me. SMASH!

It was an unwise move of *'Chicken Lickin'* proportions and the full force of the menu came careering down in his face knocking him off the seat and backwards to the ground. Prity screamed, Dalj stood up aghast and Baldip looked on embarrassed by it all. Pinto in the meantime kept chomping away at her food blissfully unaware of the commotion around her and firmly entranced in her own bubble.

I dropped the menu, complete with smeared fly next to number 54 – Chicken Jal-fly-zi and rushed to assist Spiros to get him back to his feet.

What happened next knocked the stuffing out of me as Spiros grabbed me by the lapels and threw me to the ground next to him and began punching and biting me in equal measure. I struggled to shake him off but he was far too strong for me and the blows rained in without any reasoning. The others tried to intervene, but struggled due to the ferocious manner of his intent to hurt me for humiliating him in such a denigrating way.

As we lay there and he bit me for the last time on my shoulder he moved his face close to mine and quietly hissed, 'By the end of this trip I will get that part you mongrel, remember what I said.'

He then stood up and dusted himself down and even stretched out his hand to help me up.

Prity helped me to my feet and we all sat down. I could see Baldip frantically explaining that everything was okay to the restaurant staff who had all watched in shock at the violent caberet that was played out for their delectation.

The remainder of the lunch was eaten in utter silence with the flies sitting around and tucking into my Chicken dish, complete with napkins and knives and forks due to the lack of resistance from anyone after the episode we had just endured. Other flies were meanwhile circling the menu with their hats in their hands chanting a prayer for their fly buddy who had been killed in action with his tongue hanging out of his splattered mouth.

A short while later we settled the bill and Baldip drove us to the beach where we soaked up the sea breeze and tried to relax. The bite marks from Spiros throbbed and were timely reminders to me that my Bollywood dream was in extremis and my hopes were perilously close to being crushed by his presence.

Pinto set off down the beach and rolled up her suit so that she could soak up the waves on her hairy legs.

Baldip and Spiros walked off together and stood some distance away from us. They seemed as though they were deep in conversation about something. Spiros was animated with his arms as Baldip seemed to be listening attentively. I could not hear what was being said, but did notice at one stage that Baldip placed his arm around the shoulder of Spiros. I told Prity to look and she shrugged her shoulders and said, 'Honestly, I don't trust that Baldip as far as I can throw him. There is something fishy about him.'

With that, she looked back out at the direction of the sea.

I then noticed Spiros apparently leaning close to Baldip and I saw what appeared to be money exchanging hands.

Baldip looked around and quickly placed the money in his trouser pocket and they then walked off along the beach away from us, with the breaking waves crashing at their feet. I looked on pensively and was not sure what had just happened, but something was not right.

I tried to relax my mind for the first time since arriving. My mind had been a tumultuous rollercoaster of emotions and sights and I knew that I had this day to chill out, soak up the rays and then hopefully make sweet and tender love to Prity that evening, before the real work started in the morning.

The threat of Spiros and now the suspicion of duplicity from Baldip were two factors that were laying heavily on my mind as I sat there with Prity in-between my legs on the sand. Dalj was a short distance away from us looking out wistfully into the sea, his trousers rolled up to his knees. I noticed that he kept fidgeting and shuffling his legs about. He must have changed positions over twenty times in the short time that I was looking at him.

'Dalj, have you got ants in your pants?' I shouted across to him.

He looked at me concentrated and full of anguish.

'What's the matter mate, you cool? I sat up as did Prity.

'I think I have got food poisoning mate. I have got the shits.' he replied weakly.

Prity started to laugh like a hyena and I followed suit. Dalj suddenly stood up with a mysterious brown residue trickling down his leg and on to the golden sand.

'He has got Delhi belly,' screamed an unsympathetic Prity.

'Where is the nearest toilet, where? His voice was laced with desperation and plight. He shuffled on the spot, his eyes scanning the beach for signs of a toilet.

I stood up and looked around but could not find one. Prity's face suddenly turned to abject horror when she noticed the brown residue leaking from his trousers.

'He has done it in his...'

'Not now.' Dalj cut Prity off and ran off like Zola Budd in her heyday. He raced up the beach with breathtaking speed, beating all land speed records as he sought out a throne somewhere, anywhere to unload the burden in his pants. No such luck. He raced back to us, his face like thunder and desperate.

I did not know what to suggest as the brown watery poo snaked down even more embarrassingly.

Dalj suddenly stripped off his trousers and tossed them to the ground before darting off towards the water before lunging in both feet first as he immersed himself. We looked on in shock, surely he was not going to...

Dalj swam out further and then turned to face us. His face contorting, twisting, and then relaxing completely in sheer relief as a bubble of brown water suddenly appeared and surrounded his head, caressing his neck and face in grim confirmation that he had soiled himself. The tiny splashes of brown water sloshed up to his face and into his mouth causing him to gag.

Both Prity and I went to retch but nothing came out. Dalj stayed in the water for twenty minutes before he built up the confidence to return and face the music from us. Meanwhile Baldip and Spiros returned and were one step away from holding hands with their newly formed friendship. If Baldip had just buggered Spiros then he had done the job well as Spiros sported a cheesy grin. Pinto also joined us and appeared more relaxed and content from her time spent at the beach.

Baldip then drove us back to the hotel and said that he would pick us up in the morning.

Before leaving and out of earshot to everyone else I pulled Baldip to one side. My dad had always taught me to ask things outright if you had a problem with someone and here I sought my opportunity. I whispered, 'Is there anything that you want to tell me Baldip?'

He checked my expression and lowered his eyes to the floor.

He looked guilty about something but I could not identify exactly what it was.

'No problem Sam saab. Everything is good. You enjoy India so far?' He moved his head side to side a few times in succession, an Asian mannerism indicating friendliness and hospitality. I was not convinced.

At first, he remained a closed book and no amount of questioning or coaxing bought me any closer to nailing the root problem and my suspicion. Our conversation then lasted some twenty minutes and mainly revolved around me telling him my life story and uphill struggle that I had endured to get to where I was today. He too shared his feelings about our arrival in India and his opinions on me, and the others in my entourage. He looked as though he took it all in and our getting to know one another discussion was fruitful. He then walked off telling me that he would pick me up in the morning. I walked back to the others.

Pinto said that she was going to have a siesta and Dalj took her to her room. Meanwhile Prity and I sat around the outside tables by the swimming pool at the back of the hotel. Spiros lingered nearby at the bar and looked over at us studying what we were doing.

I felt uncomfortable and wanted to spend some time with Prity but Spiros then snaked up and insisted in staying in close proximity.

Prity leaned in close to me, 'I am so glad that I am here with you baby. You know I really love you and I know it sounds silly, but...' She stopped and shook her head.

'What's that babe? What's silly? I enquired.

'Nah, you will just laugh at me.' She appeared to be blushing.

'I promise I won't.' I could not have sounded more convincing.

'It's just that I really love you. You are the most genuine guy I have ever met, you are funny, kind and so romantic. But above all else, you don't shit your pants in the sea,' she laughed.

How sexy was my girlfriend I thought. She said all that without any prompting from me and my chest puffed with pride. I hugged her close to me and kissed her on the forehead. I had the best prize ever with me right now and success in Bollywood was just a bonus I thought.

Our conversation ebbed and flowed and we reminisced about the times before we met and previous girlfriends. I had certainly had my fair share of monsters and Quasimodo type critters that I had dated before landing the jackpot with Prity.

I remembered one such filly a few years back. The monster had somehow slithered into my life when my guard was pulled down. We were manacled together for two grisly weeks and the only lasting memories I had from her were a bout of crabs and VD. Her humongous tattooed jugs gave me my first indications that she was not the kind of girl who you would invite home for a spot of tea. I mean you know something is not right when the girl you are with sprouts more facial hair than you. I gave her the big heave-ho after our relationship hit the skids, and I praised the Lord that her or the tattooed jugs never darkened my hall again.

Another time there was this monstrosity who insisted on wanting to make out with me every time I visited the after school gym, I mean come on 'ughhhh.' She actually got off when I smeared my skunk like sweat over her face. Needless to say, that particular relationship lasted a matter of weeks before she was cut out of my life. I never saw her after that but guessed she had been locked up for experiments in some institution somewhere.

However, my overall favourite creature from the depths of Hell was this buck toothed stunt that I had met at a party several months before Prity came down from the clouds like an angel. She had teeth the size of the white cliffs of Dover and her carrot crunching ways did not improve my self esteem one bit when people would shout out the cruellest things like 'Oh look there goes Elma Fudd and Bugs,' when we were seen out together. Our relationship was doomed from the outset and fizzled out accordingly.

Spiros had now left the pool area and had walked off somewhere.

We chatted some more and I knew she sure was one of a kind, a really different and special girl.

Prity laughed as she recalled a time during our courtship. This was one time when Prity had invited me to a family function where she had asked me to dress up in a traditional manner stating that it would score me brownie points in the future. So, what did I do? I got Karpal – Dalj's father to tie a turban on me and dress me in a traditional white Indian kurta pyjama outfit. This was a recipe for disaster. The function was Prity's auntie's birthday and here I was clean shaven, wearing an overgrown Indian suit with the sleeves hanging over my hands and creases rolled up by my ankles from the trousers being too long. I had also been given some curled up shoes called mojaay to wear, not to mention my turban had tilted over to one side therefore covering one ear and not the other. I looked like a sack of shit but I was there to impress them with the thought of my efforts for the girl I love. BIG MISTAKE!

As soon as I walked in, I was instantaneously ripped to shreds by everyone. The guests thought that I was some kind of comedian that they had booked to entertain the guests. I looked like a page out of the Arabian knights. The little kids at the party rinsed me for every joke under the sun and the coup de grace for me was when I had to bend down and touch the feet of the head of the house as Prity had showed me beforehand and pay my respects to them in this traditional manner. Well it all went Pete Tong when in the excitement of it all I lunged down at the first auntie I came across and touched her feet. The nauseating stench of cheese, peeling corns, and eau de bunion making me retch. Auntie Balwant's feet were the answer to curing the foot fetish fever that millions around the globe had harboured. I mean if you sucked on those babies you'd be lying on your back in a coma for a long time to come. I glanced up at her husband standing obediently by her side and immediately solved the riddle of cold sores that were covering his mouth. I felt a shiver run down my spine that had me instantaneously traumatised. I felt myself choking out as I shot back up to my feet, light headed and in need of some much needed air.

My turban had now shifted to the other side of my head and was barely hanging on by a thread or two. I did not have time to adjust it as Prity pinched my arm and positioned me in front of the real McCoy and the auntie whose party it actually was.

I went down to touch her feet and pay my respects and heard a rip. I looked around anxiously and saw that the tail of my kurta pyjama jacket had got caught in the door behind me and had ripped. From my bent position I felt aunties hand patting my head like I was some kind of dog, either that or she was knighting me. In my petulance I yanked my head up quickly and my turban went flying off of my head and through the living room window and out into the street. Auntie and the rest of the guests looked at me in disgust. Suffice to say that the party was relatively short for me and I was ushered home with my turban under my arm and Prity not seeing the funny side of it.

They were funny times we both laughed, the kind of rib tickling humour when no sound comes out of your mouth for a few seconds. I looked up and saw Dalj walking towards us.

'Hey guys. What's so funny? You still laughing about my incident?' he asked curiously.

'Yeah now that is what I call an arse burner.' I laughed raucously. It wasn't that funny but it was a case of having the giggles and frankly he could have said anything and we would have laced him for it with a comedic spin. Dalj did not look amused.

'Ha ha, very funny mate. That curry was roasting hot bruv. I could have shit through the eye of a needle I tell ya,' Dalj lightened the mood by mocking himself.

'I know, don't worry shit happens,' Prity chipped in with timely levity and we all chuckled again.

'What you chatting about anyway?' Dalj probed.

'Nah, we were just talking about the times when we were courting and stuff.' I put him at ease.

'Listen mate I am just going to get some indigestion tablets from outside, so I'll catch you for a drink in a minute.' Dalj turned to walk.

'Wait Dalj. You have done a lot for me. Let me go. I could do with the leg stretch.' I insisted and told Dalj to chill out by the pool while I went to get the tablets he required.

Dalj ordered a drink and kicked back as I went out into the chaotic hustle and bustle of Mumbai's streets.

What I had not realised in my innocence was that the Grim Reaper was sharpening his scythe and waiting for the moment when I was on my own, and now he had his window of opportunity. The road ahead was perilous and full of deadly and life ending land mines. I ventured out into the street, alone and unaware, not realising that I may never make it back…

Chapter 7

Mumbai dangerous

I had been walking now for about five minutes, crossing the busy streets and negotiating the swarming traffic risking life, limb and sanity in the process. Suddenly my eyes beamed in delight when I saw a chemist sign up in the distance. I walked on towards it satisfied that I would be able to get some medication to help my good friend. The whirr of traffic peppered the air, the incessant revving of engines and tooting of horns was ever present and in a way I was kind of getting used to it by now.

There were literally hundreds of darned auto rickshaws strewn about the street and others sweeping past me carrying tourists and locals to their destinations. Auto rickshaws or three wheeler, pedicab, bug, cyclo are one of the most prevalent and popular modes of transport where there is regular traffic congestion in a city. Rickshaws' first appeared in Japan around 1868 at the beginning of the Meiji restoration and were invented by an American missionary, whereby he designed it to transport his invalid wife Yokohoma about. It quickly gained recognition and became a widely used and faster method of transportation than some of the more conventional means. The word rickshaw actually derived from the Japanese word, 'Jinriksha' meaning human powered vehicle, just think Flintstones and you are getting there.

I continued walking down the street whilst soaking up the rays of the morning sun when I heard the mosquito like purring of a rickshaw seemingly very close behind me. I did not look around as this was a common sound in this part of the world and just expected it to whizz past me.

I was several feet away from the chemists and just as I was about to walk up the short ramp leading to the front door I was aware that the revving rickshaw noise became louder and louder. I turned suddenly and recoiled in horror as the rickshaw mounted the low kerb and shot towards me at break neck speed. I instinctively staggered back quickly losing my footing on some concrete slabs lying by the roadside. The rickshaw headed right towards my fallen carcass with menacing promise. The driver was a blurred vision due to the sun rays bouncing off the window. I was dead meat and could see the chunky front wheel hammering towards my legs without a shred of doubt as to what the driver's intent was. I lay there stunned like a rodent in the headlights of a truck. If I did not lose my legs in this freakish road traffic accident then I would almost certainly die from the loss of all six pints of my blood from the wounds the jagged edge of the wheel would leave. At least my friends back in the UK would have subsequently believed my horror stories of Mumbai's driving conditions when I regaled them in the pub with my stories, having the ability to be authenticated as I ripped off my prosthetic legs to slake their ghoulish appetites.

Heart frozen and head spinning in a web of imminent terror, I could see that the rickshaw was seconds away from chopping off my legs. BANG! In what can only be described as serendipity and sheer fox like reflexes I pulled my legs quickly and violently towards my chest and off the ground, causing me to stumble even further backwards. The rickshaw violently smacked directly into the space where I had been laying and where I would almost certainly have lost my legs. The front wheel smashed unceremoniously into the raised concrete slabs with ferocious intent. As a result, the rickshaw tipped viciously to one side flying off into the air past me and came smashing down on the ground, skidding for several yards in a crumpled heap.

A crowd of rubber-neckers and passers by quickly gathered and helped me to my feet. They were babbling away in Hindi too frenetically for me to actually apply my linguistic skills and understand or decipher what was being said.

I looked down and checked to see if my legs were still intact. Thankfully they were. I flexed them once or twice just to assure myself and breathed a sigh of relief as the beasts were fully functional.

I slowly shuffled over to the sideward's turned rickshaw with the front wheel still spinning uncontrollably.

I had to see if the driver was okay. It was obviously a case of the rickshaw malfunctioning at the last minute and the driver not being able to steer it away from me. I was sure that this kind of incident was rife in the troubled driving conditions of the sprawling metropolis of Mumbai.

The passers by all heaved and puffed as they pushed the rickshaw back to how it should be, mumbling amongst one another and speaking in hushed tones. The driver inside rattled and shook from side to side, like a car crash dummy as they lifted the rickshaw back to its original position. I could see that he had a trickle of blood on his hands and some cuts and bruises.

I stood back and could not quite get to him to assess his condition due to the crowd of helpers who had encircled the accident.

I rubbed my hand as I had landed heavily on it when I fell back and worked my fingers to regain the flex and motion in them once again.

Suddenly. I heard a rumpus taking place by the rickshaw. I heard screams of despair and shouting. I looked over nervously. Maybe the driver was going into some kind of post traumatic shock, or had suffered internal injuries that were just beginning to surface.

'Call an ambulance quick!' I shouted as I moved towards the front of the crowd.

I then heard the crunching of bones and smashing of jaws as passer by after passer by was thrown back out of the crowd where they fell to the floor injured and in agonising pain on the sidewalk. I will never forget the look of terror emblazoned on their little mugs (faces) as victim suddenly became aggressor and hunted became hunter, welcoming the bunch of budding Florence Nightingale folks into a cornucopia of pain.

The driver emerged from the wreck punching, kicking and head butting several more gatherers before focussing on me, his eyes burning like the fires of Hell. I shuffled back in sheer terror. The driver was...ANIL! The cunning predator had tracked me down to India, and now here he was trying to maim me. There were only certain things that scared me to my very core in life and they were, lions, tigers, bears...and Anil.

'Don't worry you piece of shit. I won't kill you just yet. Not until I get hold of the money that you owe me.' He snarled as he tasted the blood on his hand - Bruce Lee style before looking back at my scrawny little frame.

He then reached behind his back and pulled out a long deadly looking knife, and pointed it at me.

'What's the matter you want a piece of my little friend?' His words would not have looked out of place in a horror movie.

'I am going to quench my thirst with your blood.' This dude was not acting and meant every slithering word. He stepped forward and I could taste the aura of malevolence in the air.

I gulped so hard I could actually feel my balls shrivelling so far up inside my body that I actually tasted them in my mouth.

The crowd dispersed in every direction, screaming and shouting like they were in some kind of disaster film. I stood firm for a moment or two while I surveyed the options available to me. Whimper like a baby and then get stabbed, shit my pants and then get stabbed or promise to foot rub him every day and then still get…you guessed it – stabbed. I looked on like the gift wrapped turd that I was in contemplative doom. What did this banjo strumming hill billy want with me?

'Now you know what time it is? Be sensible and choose your next response very carefully. Where is my money?' He twirled the knife and stepped in closer towards me trying to smoke out the blood money from me.

I froze and had visions of the knife poking out of the back of me. I was afraid and very much caught in the spider's web. I could not understand how he had tracked me down to Mumbai. It was impossible, just impossible for him to have done that. It was the moment I would discover whether this hyped up good boy turned gangster was actually the real paragon of iniquity or just full of piss, snot and hot air.

I remained silent, more from the shock of everything rather than some dignified stand against tyranny and turpitude. Sod that shit I thought, this was about self preservation and looking after numero uno.

'Oh, so you don't want to give me the money. Fuck it. I am gonna cut you so that you can reflect this evening and then make a wiser choice when I see you tomorrow. COME HERE!' He growled and lunged at me with his grasping and bloodied paw.

I danced to one side with deft aplomb, I was the mongoose and he was the snake, and before I knew what was happening I was involved in the most insane foot chase ever, skipping and sliding over vehicles like Starsky and Hutch. I dodged rickshaws by a mere whisker and skipped around the gazillions of sheep like people who seemed to be walking around aimlessly in the sunshine. I did not have any idea where I was running to but ran as fast as my little feet could muster. Every time I looked behind me I saw the hulking frame of Anil cruising a safe distance but gaining ground all the while. He seemed to be gliding effortlessly and rattled my senses. Who the hell was he, the flaming Energiser Bunny? I feared.

After several more near misses, I managed to give him the slip and made it into a hotel out of the vision of Anil and I remained there for a good few hours as I waited for the dust to settle. I had made the required goal line clearance today by escaping with my limbs still attached to my body, but would need to be on championship form to keep the predator from hunting me down, that was a certainty.

My hands were shaking like the proverbial leaves and my guts had been twisted and churned from the brush with death that I just had. What possessed him to come all the way to India to finish me off? Did he not realise that I had already had my lifetime's worth of bad luck and hardship to contend with?

As the afternoon sun slowly crept behind the clouds and the crimson winds of anger had dissipated for the time, I decided that it was time to emerge from my hiding place and make my way back to the hotel. I crept in and out of the shadows of the night, using the building line where I could to sneak back to the hotel unscathed. Alas, I had made it. I searched the lobby nervously and waited patiently before coming out from behind the pot plant when I was certain the coast was clear. In the hotel room I sat on the bed as Prity showered me with a slew of questions about my whereabouts along with accompanying kisses and heartfelt hugs. I took some time to compose myself and quaffed a few Jack Daniels from the mini-bar before regaling her with the warts and all representation of what dread and imperilment I had just suffered. As usual, her comforting words were the perfect aphrodisiac to assuage and expunge any further hurt from my haggard existence.

I lay back on the bed and spoke cautiously, 'I am scared, really scared. I just don't know what is happening to me. There are so many evil and jealous people out here, who all want to see me suffer. They want to steal from me, humiliate me and take what little shred of hope that I have left. Why?' I asked my soul mate for the answers to my rhetorical questions. I had not even noticed a pool of tears that had formed on the floor beside my shoes. The kind of tears that don't even roll down your cheeks, but just freefall with gushing accuracy in the same spot. My throat was heavy and croaky and my voice squeaked some more, 'What do I have to do to get some happiness in my life?'

I looked at Prity for some guidance and she kissed my forehead and squeezed me tight.

'Don't worry okay. I am here. You just keep doing the right thing and it will be okay.' She sure knew what buttons to press and when.

I smiled to myself knowingly and nodded my head. I knew she was right. It had all become clear to me, crystal clear, a moment of sheer lucidity and one that would pay dividends one day.

'What about calling the police?' Prity pulled away from me and held my shoulders, a light bulb turning on in her head.

'No a true hero doesn't do that. I need to deal with these small issues myself. These guys are just leeches who will move on to something else once things settle down, that is all.' It appeared from the trepidation in my own voice that I was not only trying to convince her, but myself at the same time.

The lights in my *'Bollywood Vegas'* had started to dim for me, and Anil was the fucker bringing prohibition to my shores.

'Well stuff it let's go home then. There is no way that you should suffer anymore than you need to. I can't take it. I am going to pack.' Prity moved off the bed and started to pack her suitcase by throwing her things in haphazardly. She was crying and muttering how it was not fair and that she could not understand why those gangsters as she liked to call them could not leave us to live our life in peace.

I walked up and placed my arms around her and said, 'Look you know you are not going home don't you?'

She turned and looked at me quizzically, 'Why?'

'Because my dear you would never pack that way and that is a fact. You are too organised.'

She laughed and punched me before asking, 'You sure you are okay though? I will stay only if you are happy. Are you?'

'Yes, because you are here by my side.'

We kissed and then hugged. However, I managed to disguise my inner turmoil from her with clandestine aplomb as I looked out of the window concerned and inwardly devastated. I daren't show her my true feelings and she did not realise that the whole situation frightened me to my core and I was not even sure how I would escape the imminent danger that I was in…alive. It was just impossible and we both knew it deep down!

Chapter 8

A taste of Bollywood

Tuesday 14th July – Baldip arrived at the hotel once again in timely fashion. He was dressed in a suit and had his hair viciously swept over to one side with enough Brylcream to drown a cat with.

The usual procedure was adopted with a knock on our respective rooms before being told to meet in reception.

Prity and I took the lift down from our top floor room and walked into the reception area where we saw the others standing there in sharp suits and looking immaculately groomed. Even Pinto was looking decidedly tasty strutting her stuff in her white suited chunni and garms as she revelled in her 80 – 90 wrinklies' holiday. She flirted shamelessly with the waiters despite being several generations above them. The waiters seemed okay with her behaviour, probably because she had a pulse and some of her own teeth, so was game in their eyes. There were a collection of buns and some orange juice which we all enjoyed as our breakfast.

Baldip was talking feverishly on the phone. He was pacing up and down the floor and I could hear him saying to whoever was on the other end of the line that he had the best two newbie actors in town. The conversation was quite animated and it appeared that he was talking to one of the Bollywood big wigs. He mentioned Spiros and me several more times and then concluded the phone call.

Prity turned to me and said sticking her snout in the trough, 'Like I said to you before I don't trust that guy. You mark my words he is bad news. Look at his eyes they are evil.'

'Yeah but why would he do me any harm?' I whispered quietly to her.

'These Indian's are all after your money, trust me I know them too well. He has got wind that you have got money and he will be sniffing around it like the kuta (dog) he is.' I had never seen Prity so vociferous as she was, and quite frankly her prediction was scary.

I looked at her and then at Baldip and in particular his eyes. She was right they were laced with malevolence and evil forces. Oh God I mused dejectedly, not another enemy in my midst. That is all I needed.

Baldip pranced over to us and started to babble something about showing us around the Bollywood film studios, and how he had just secured some passes to enable us to do this.

'Now your auditions are not until tomorrow but you will get a taste of the industry today. If you have any questions then please feel free to ask. I will also introduce you to Jaspal Verma, the movie mogul and chief director,' he said to us.

Spiros looked genuinely happy and excited. He then patted me on the back and muttered, 'Best of luck comrade,' before skulking off behind Baldip to the minibus. Pinto followed Dalj outside and Prity and I held up the rear.

After half an hour of more near death experiences on the streets of Mumbai we arrived at one of the main and most majestic and grandeur Bollywood film studios. The resplendent and verdant gardens that led to the brick built haven depicted its true magnificence. Bollywood does not exist as a physical place unlike Hollywood, but is the area where the Asian films are produced. Bollywood's film production centre is a government owned studio facility known as 'Film City' in the northern suburbs of Mumbai. This was the budding actor's nirvana and here I was frothing like a Labrador studying the sheer indulgent magnificence of such a Disneyland type venue.

With up to fourteen million Indians going to the movies on a daily basis, paying the equivalent of their average day's wages to see any one of the thousand or so movies churned out each year, it was where I wanted to make my name. I was aware of other white actors such as the well known Tom Alter and Bob Christo to name but a few who had treaded this path previously. I knew I had the credentials and stamina for this challenge and was hoping to seize my opportunity when it came.

Even though India is the country where up to sixteen official languages are spoken along with other dialects spoken by millions of other inhabitants, it is still Bollywood the largest film industry in the world that attracts the masses from every walk of life to its captivating Hindi movies. The movies were guaranteed to provide three or four hours of true escapism as its primary objective, allowing the people from the slums and harsh poverty ridden lives to indulge in the 'masala' that these films provide in abundance.

Other nearby facets of Bollywood include Chennai (formerly known as Madras) where they produce films in Tamil. Then there is Kolkata (formerly known as Calcutta) which is the Bengali film capital and furthermore neighbouring Pakistan which is fondly known as Lollywood. All of the industries have one ingredient baked right in with the cherry on top for added measure and that is to wow the audience and allow the viewer to vicariously enjoy the life of his or her dreams. It is as simplistic as that.

Baldip started to tell us of the history of the wonderful Bollywood industry with the landmark on the 7th July 1896 when a movie was shown for the first time. He stated that some time later in 1913 the first Indian silent movie was shown, a movie called 'Raja Harishchandra,' based on the Mahabharata. I found myself wildly interested in the history lesson as he was delving into areas for which I had not one iota of knowledge. He chirped on like the frustrated tourist rep that he was and explained that the first movie with sound was shot in 1931, a movie called 'Alam Ara,' and this was an instant super hit. Despite these early signs of future global success and ascendency, he also mentioned the 1930's and 1940's were harsh times in India due to the Great Depression, World War 2, the Indian Independence Movement, and the Partition.

The colours, muscles and melodrama were then slowly introduced in the 1950's with such greats as Raj Kapoor, Dilip Kumar and Dev Anand creating their legendary and indelible marks. The 1960's saw the emergence of other classic action stars such as Amitabh Bachchan, Dharmendra, Jeetendra and Rajesh Khanna. The 1980's and 1990's were the breeding ground for some red hot masterpieces' of cinema viewing. Finally he added In the 2000's there was a substantial growth in the film industry and this led to spectacular filmmaking including enhanced special effects, improved quality, better cinematography and technical advances in all aspects of the movie process.

'And now you will have the classic birth of the next all conquering action hero, me Spiros – the half Greek, half Italian warrior bursting on to a screen near you soon.' Spiros held his arms up in the air triumphantly much to everyone's scowling and dismay.

'Welcome to the promised land friends. Beinvenido to Bollywood.' A well groomed man speaking with an obviously fake posh accent walked towards us with his arms out stretched as we got out of the minibus. I recoiled at the sight of his greasy jet black hair draped firmly over his skull and sitting on top of his oily and well rounded face. I noticed his small, slanted eyes squinting from the rays of the sun as he traipsed towards us, shuffling his portly and rotund frame up the gravel with purpose.

'Mr Verma. How are you?' Baldip shook his hand and then introduced us to this reputable director. The guy that stood there with the ticket to fulfilling all of my dreams.

'Hmm. Who is this?' Jaspal walked behind me looking me up and down and peering over my shoulder subtly just like the witch in Chitty Chitty Bang Bang.

'Sam Miers from England,' I mumbled respectfully.

His presence was unfamiliar and slightly disconcerting I thought as he moved on to identify Dalj, Pinto and Prity. He stopped at Spiros and gave him the same kind of lubricious and lecherous leer that he had given me.

We all exchanged concerned looks with one another as Jaspal then smiled and beckoned us to follow him. We walked through some double doors and past the reception desks into another room.

It was here that we were offered refreshments and a chance to ask questions about the auditions process. All my concerns were allayed satisfactorily and Jaspal provided pithy answers all the time.

'You have been selected because you are two of the best that Grooving Singhs's Drama School has to offer. I have seen some tapes of you boys and I must say that you both look even better in the flesh.'

His *Blue Oyster Club* type grin that accompanied that statement made me grimace.

Despite his bizarre mannerisms, I noticed that Spiros continually sucked up to Jaspal all throughout the initial meet and greet, including when he showed us around the various studios within the vast industry. This was the home of film making and we were at the very nucleus of it.

Prity commented, 'I am getting sick to death of his yes sir, no sir, three bags full sir rubbish. I mean how much more of his bullshit can we take.' Prity was right in her assessment and Spiros really was the aficionado and quintessential brown nosing champ of the world.

The pace of the day moved very quickly and before I knew it we were left to wander around ourselves just to get a feel for the place. Baldip began to explain where various famous Bollywood movies had been shot including who starred in them. I noticed from the corner of my eye that Dalj had taken a fancy to one of the dancing girls. There were a group of them practicing their moves behind us in step with the barking instructions from the Sonder Kommando, a.k.a. - the drill instructor. This particular girl kept giving Dalj the eye and smiling and I could see that the old fellow was getting quite excited by it all.

'Lunch time,' was shouted out by the drill instructor and the dancing girls began to shift away in smaller groups where they would enjoy the delights of the nearby sandwich bar using their well earned rupees to satiate their rumbling stomachs. This one girl, with metaphorical balls the size of melons smiled and walked straight over to Dalj without a seconds thought. Dalj was visibly cringing and in an attempt to look cool he started to fumble around with some flowers hanging from a nearby tree and started to stroke the stem before accidentally pricking himself on a thorn in the process, yelping as he did so.

'What the hell is he doing?' I asked Prity. She just looked on patently embarrassed for Dalj.

The young girl then walked up to him as he bumbled around like Inspector Clueless and they engaged in small talk. We looked on in admiration with Pinto clapping her hands and seemingly skipping on the dusty floor in what looked like geriatric Bhangra. She looked good for her age and I was impressed.

After a few moments they broke away and Dalj tried to look casual as he strolled back over to us. He was not convincing anyone and I could tell that the little butterflies in his stomach were doing cartwheels inside.

'Oi oi, what's happened there Daljy boy?' I asked.

'Nah, nothing. She wants to meet me when she knocks off in a couple of hours.' He looked sheepish about his hot date. I don't know why because from the angle that I had seen her, she looked quite nice.

We spent the next few hours walking around and introducing ourselves to other small time actors and part timers. It was fun and I now felt more relaxed with it all. I had decided that I would simply act the way I knew best and let the director make the final call to assess if I was good enough or not. I refused to allow Spiros to intimidate me with his presence or threats. What could he have done to me if the director chose me over him? It was not as though it would be my fault. I could always say that I was under acting like Spiros had warned me to do so but the director still picked me if that was the case. But, I knew that saying all this was one thing but the execution was a different ball game altogether. The road ahead was pit fallen and arduous.

The end of filming at Bollywood was here and the actors and dancers started to go home. There were no night shoots on this occasion and therefore things were being closed down after a frenetic day's activity. Jaspal popped his head out through the double doors and shouted,' See you tomorrow for the first audition and hey you are all invited to my house afterwards for a small party that I am having, okay.'

With that, he disappeared into the studios as we waved goodbye and extended our thanks for his hospitality.

All of a sudden, Dalj's hot date emerged from the other side, near the dancer's barracks or changing rooms and beckoned him over. I saw Baldip smirking and telling him that we would wait for him at the café across the road, and not to be longer than one hour or we would leave without him. Dalj gave the thumbs up and darted off with new found confidence to his beauty queen.

The pair of them linked hands and snuck off into one of the barracks where they would be able to get some privacy.

'Wow, I guess the girls in India move fast. I am impressed.' I said to the others. 'None of this getting to know each other phase. A simple case of let's see if we are compatible in the sack then ask questions later type of scenario. I like it.' I addressed all of them.

'Oh I think your friend will be pleasantly surprised alright.' Baldip chortled to himself.

We ordered some drinks and it was when they were being served some ten minutes later that I noticed Dalj come racing back to us as though his life depended upon it. His trousers were dangling down from his waist and he had a look of complete horror etched all over his mush. We all stood up concerned apart from Baldip, who continued to stir his tea smug and unmoved by the obvious danger that Dalj was in.

He made it over to us sweating and dishevelled, stumbling on to the seat while quickly tying up his trouser belt. He was out of breath and in-between pants began to mumble,' She...IT has got one.'

He searched around for some answers with his eyes, but none were forthcoming.

'Got what?' Spiros asked confused.

'Yeah, what's he talking about?' Prity sounded miffed by it all.

'IT...has got a fucking dick,' he muttered confused and equally shell shocked by the trauma.

'She, IT, that thing started kissing me and then as we were getting into it I reached down and found it. The bitch! I was set up by it.' Dalj's face was a picture.

I tried my utmost to stifle my laughter as did Prity. We looked at Baldip and he said, 'She was a beauty QUEEN alright.' That was it the three of us laughed uncontrollably. Dalj lashed out at us but we dodged his strikes with body swerves and laughed some more. Pinto looked on happy in her bubble and incognizant as to what was going on around her as per usual. Spiros meanwhile looked at Dalj and snarled, 'You stupid fool. You think any proper girl would like twice at you. Muppet!' He looked away disgusted.

'Hey, leave him alone. It is none of your business.' I shouted across at Spiros. I was getting sick to death of his jaundiced comments and abusive behaviour and was not afraid to voice my opinion to him.

'Oh, talking of dicks. What do you want again?' His repartee was clinical and hard to follow.

'Yeah, well I will do my talking at the audition tomorrow. Then we will see who the dick is.' I felt brave in the company that I had and knew that he would be foolish to lash out at me with so many witnesses especially as I had not physically hit him such as the demon fly incident. I was right. He just sniffed his nostrils hard and looked away.

After all the commotion of the past few days events it all boiled down to the auditions tomorrow and the following days to decide if I had the substance and kahoonas to be involved in the majestical Bollywood film industry. We trudged back to the minibus and I placed my arm around the shoulder of Dalj, the poor blighter he was certainly accumulating some infamous memories of his time in India.

I managed to take a sly look at Spiros and at Baldip as we walked, and knew that around the pair of them I would have to have my guard well and truly up or otherwise the end would be nigh for my dreams and possibly my life with treachery abounding with such villainous intent in my midst.

Chapter 9

Wolf at the door

It had been a long and weary few days and we had all agreed that we would retire early in preparation for the auditions tomorrow morning. Pinto looked tired and shifted her weary bones up the stairs (the lift was temporarily out of service). I could actually hear her bones creaking and groaning with every step. It was sad to see and I was afraid deep down that the excitement of the trip, coupled with her age may be the triggers for some kind of heart attack or stroke. It worried me and we all helped her up the stairs to her room where she went to sleep on her bed.

'You okay mate?' I asked Dalj.

He smiled back at me, 'Just about I tell you.'

He had always been there for me and so I leaned forward and hugged him. It was not a very manly thing to do but not only did I feel sorry for the guy, it was one of those moments in life where nothing other than a big, fat, juicy hug would have sufficed, and I guess that was the best way of showing my appreciation.

Prity and I retired back to our room and closed the door. I went to kiss her and she hesitated at first complaining of a headache and as I leaned in she moved her head away at the last minute, she had been watching too many Bollywood films I guess. I was half expecting her to run behind the cupboard in one suit and come out wearing another just to get my juices flowing like a feral Mustang horse.

After several more whimsical attempts by me she gave it up for some flesh on flesh trouser action as I figured she would when I dialled the right buttons. She started to kiss me passionately ripping at my clothing with purpose - after all, she was only human. I did not stop her and reciprocated. We were getting into the throes of passion with my body aching for hers. Just as we fell on to the bed with her straddling me I heard the faint sound of knocking on the door. Prity looked up and then back at me, 'Just ignore that, it is probably Spiros looking to wind you up again or something.' She continued to kiss me. The knocks became louder and I moved Prity gently off of me and sat up.

'It might be important. I will see what he wants.' I said standing up and heading towards the door. Prity draped the duvet around her voluptuous body and whispered,' Make it quick. I need you to make me feel like a woman.'

In cartoon type fashion my legs flapped quickly in the air for several seconds before I raced off to the door to get rid of the unwelcome guest and get on with making out with my girl.

I opened the door and saw nothing, nada. I popped my head outside and still there was emptiness.

I mumbled a few expletives under my breath and then turned to walk back in the room, 'There is no-one there. Some idiot is playing a....'

BANG! Before I knew what was happening I felt a blow to the back of my head which caused me to fall face first on to the floor. The pain seared through my body. I tried to turn on the floor rather like a wounded slug but saw little birds circling above my head. An immediate ripple of fear and unease could be felt around the room and I was not sure what was coming next in this unpredictable situation.

I heard Prity screaming and vaguely saw her being pushed back on the bed. Her scream felt physical and reverberated around the small room. She was determined and fought back against the intruder with all her might. Through the haziness and blurred vision I could see her being slapped several times before finally slumping back on the bed where she appeared to be crying hysterically and cowering in fear.

I shuffled on to my elbows and tried to focus on the enemy who was trying to take what little I had left in life. All I could see was that the assailant was wearing all black clothing and had their face obscured by a black hood.

The faceless intruder then lunged forward and kicked me one final time in the head knocking me a few feet backwards. Luckily for me at this stage I had not sustained any permanent damage or facial injuries which would have meant instant dismissal from the audition process.

Once again, I gathered myself and glanced over to Prity. She sat there petrified and shaking uncontrollably. She was clutching the side of her face where she was slapped, her eyes were pleading for me to extricate her from this quagmire that she had found herself embroiled in with me. It was not her fault and now here she was in the maelstrom of violence for just being a supportive partner.

'Get to your feet and sit down you fucking shambles.' The intruder spoke and I complied, slowly and in great discomfort. I perched myself on the edge of the bed and held Prity's hand. The voice sounded familiar and then the attacker took his hood off. It was Anil. He had found me once again. His connections would be on course to earn handsome bonuses for their G.P.S. type proficiency in locating my every movement.

The reality of the danger that I had found myself in was startlingly real to me, more so than anyone else I felt guilty for Prity. What had she done to deserve this treatment? Anil was the kind of unfavourable animal that you did not want stalking you in your very own parlour. The guy was a ball of fiery anger ready to be unleashed unpredictably. He was damn ready to knock my teeth out and wear them on a chain around his neck and my next few moves had just cranked up to critical threat levels.

'You see that lovely girl. Well she won't be lovely for long if I don't get my money. You understand don't you?' His words were menacing.

Prity exchanged an anxious look with me patently wondering what hovel that Anil had crawled out from.

'I always get what I want and I will let you watch me take her before your eyes,' he fired the warning shot across the bows.

I did not know what to say. My furrowing brow and trembling lip were the only two things that I could feel due to the numbness of the entire situation being rammed home to me. Father had always said when I was a child getting bullied at school that if trouble came my way then to walk away from it alive, because pride not only hurt you, it was capable of getting you killed on the streets.

'What do you mean?' I was secretly hoping that he was not saying what I thought he was, but a picture was forming.

'You're a big boy now, so I am sure you can read between the lines.' Anil lit a cigarette and took a deep drag.

'Look just leave us alone you bastard. What do you want from him?' Prity said exasperated.

'I want my money like I said to you. So where is it? And don't insult me now.' I could feel the fires of discontent bubbling away.

I stood there moulding my response, 'The money is in the bank and I will get that to you, but I need some time.'

'Course you do sweetheart,' Anil mocked me, his eyes narrowing into slits.

'It's true, I need to arrange an appointment this week and I can get you the money you want. But, I want you to promise to leave us alone after that or...'

'Or what? I don't think you are any position to start negotiating or attempting to threaten me are you? The ruinous consequences of his voice sank any hopes of me saving face in this cauldron of despair without trace. The horror of it all was standing erect and very much had me by the short and curlies.

'How much you got on you now?' asked Anil as his eyes scanned the room.

'Not much,' I responded, my voice was like brittle glass waiting to shatter. What could I have done? My body was mentally and physically drained from the continual fighting and fear that was holding a firm grip of my testicles. They say that such a combination of fatigue makes cowards of anyone, and I had all but nailed the white flag to my mast long before.

'Just get me the money and I will get out of here,' he cut me dead in my tracks. I guess he was not one for small talk. I lifted myself off the floor and walked over slowly to my suitcase. I could see his eyes boring a hole into the back of me and watching me with hawk like precision. After a few moments of rummaging around I found some money, there was not much, approximately four hundred pounds in sterling. I coughed this up to him, my hand visibly trembling as I handed over the green to this nemesis of mine. The sudden urge to rip off his head and piss down his scrawny neck was all too real but I battled against making such a schoolboy error and one that surely would have left me nursing more than a blow to the head. Father amongst other lessons he taught me when I was growing up said that in life you have to show people you have got teeth, but Anil was a tough cookie and I was painfully aware that he had a whirlwind and violent approach to things that stood in the way of his deluded goals.

Anil walked over to me and puffed some cigarette smoke in my face, 'You have until Saturday afternoon to get me my money. I will meet you downstairs in reception. If you are not there I will rip your eyes out and stick hot pokers in your sockets,' he growled menacingly.

'Oh and don't even think about telling the authorities or I will bury you in the sand's of Mumbai where no-one will find you, and won't even bat an eyelid. Capiche!'

He then walked over to where Prity was laying. He stood over her as she looked up in stunned fear. She stared wide eyed at the beast. When suddenly he lurched downwards and took hold of her chin with one hand squeezing it with tremendous force and pulling it up to his face violently.

'Oi, leave her out of this,' I screamed moving forward instinctively with my fists clenched. I was running on empty but could not have cared less because this was a matter of principle, besides there was just no time for what if's.

Anil kissed her hard on the lips as she flayed her arms about in a bid to free herself, with her strikes merely bouncing off his body. I gritted my teeth and raised my fists. He would pay for hurting my girl. He had crossed the line. However, before I was in a position to react to the threat he then threw a demoralised Prity back on the bed and laughed like a madman.

'Do anything stupid and I will break your mouth off your face,' his threat instantly put a choke hold on any ideas I had of rescuing my damsel in distress. Yeah I know I had been rabbit fucked in my own room. He had raped me of my dignity in the most appalling manner, but like Sun Tzu said in the Art of War – *the wise man retreats and regroups but essentially lives to fight another day.* I piped down and watched Anil strut past me like King Cock. He had completed his objectives for the day and strolled out of the saloon with his spurs jangling, only to stop one more time at the door and snarl, 'Saturday in reception. You had better be there with all my money or you know what time it is.'

With that threat delivered, he disappeared. Prity leapt up and jumped on me squeezing me hard. She was crying hysterically and shaking from the devastating ordeal that we had suffered.

'I want to go home babes. I feel so ashamed and violated. I just want to go home,' she was whimpering like a sick puppy and I knew exactly how she felt. My lungs were filling up with waters of despair and I was not sure which way to turn. I was meant to have come all this way and fulfilled my lifelong ambitions. Instead, I had faced adversity at every corner. There were individuals sucking in the same air as me who were trying to repossess my life and soul in any which way they could, my strength was slowly being depleted as every second ticked by. The whole situation was about as disappointing as a fairy tale without an ending.

Prity then let go and ran into the toilet where she remained for thirty minutes or so calming her frayed nerves down from the ordeal. The cornerstone of any relationship if it is to last is being there for your partner in their time of need, and this was the crucial litmus test that we were both iron trapped in. We silently knew we would both have to depend on one another unequivocally if we were to free ourselves from the conscription of evil blackmail.

In the meantime, I stood by the window and looked out across the roof tops of Mumbai - the place where dreams are supposedly made. I knew that there was a tidal wave coming, but I was not sure whether it would knock me out or merely wet my feet such was the unpredictability of it all. My body was screaming for me to climb through the window and catapult myself to the pavement below, at least then there would be a full stop to all this nonsense in my life, that much was guaranteed. So, without further ado, I placed one foot on the ledge, followed by the other, all the while supporting myself with my hands to lever my body up and through the window. It was over. My dreams had been slowly crushed ever since I had set foot on Indian soil and I could not see any respite. This was the only way. I had been served and would rather have been savaged by

Rottweiler's then stand by and let everything l love and wanted to live for get taken away from me so coldly.

'SAM! STOP!' The sudden one hundred decibel shout almost made me jump out of my skin as I wobbled precariously on the window ledge. The shout startling me so much that I almost fell out of the window in comical fashion.

'Jesus Prity. Don't do that. I almost fell.' I could feel my heart thumping loudly against my chest.

She pulled me down to safety and we hugged. I don't think I was really going to jump but I knew that I was feeling vulnerable nevertheless.

That night I lay in bed. I could not sleep and so spent the majority of the time watching Prity drifting off and seeking sanctum in Slumber Town. Even her murmuring snores were cute I thought stroking her cheek with my fingers. A short while later and unbeknown to me I too slipped away for some much needed respite, with the hope of surviving this cesspit of trauma until the end of the week where I would have to consider handing over the money to that gutless wonder. Deep down I knew it had all gone wrong, but hey that is just the way the samosa crumbles sometimes. Tomorrow was the first audition and this was my chance to be something in life. I knew that evil and sinister forces would be working overtime to prevent me from accomplishing my dream. It is just the way things rolled for me and all I could do was hope and pray for leniency and that when it happened the finish was quick and painless.

Chapter 10

Actor's paradise

Wednesday 15th July – The day of the first audition had felt like it was an eternity away when I had first heard about it back in the UK, but now here she was in all her glory.

No more rehearsals and no more poetical waxing, this was roll the sleeves up spit and grit time.

It felt crazy. We all met up in reception and while we waited for Baldip and his minibus, I used the opportunity to fill Dalj in about what had happened to us last night. He looked concerned and repeatedly asked if we were all okay. He was like a brother to me and I could tell that he was suffering the pain vicariously. That was what set him apart from everyone else I knew back home. I was happy at least for small mercies like the fact that he had accompanied me on this trip of a supposed life time.

We walked through the large gates once again after ditching the minibus in the car park and I could see that there was a stream of people working feverishly on props and costumes near the barracks. I could see lots of dancers perfecting their moves in preparation for filming later that day.

The place was abuzz with activity and it was an amazing sight. Suddenly behind me there was a commotion and lots of people started running towards a blacked out Mercedes that was pulling up. The female onlookers started to scream and the guys all jostled for a better vantage position next to the car as it stopped near the gates. The screaming was reaching fever pitch with young and old pushing and pulling one another to catch a glimpse of this person who was sat in the car.

Then all of a sudden the door was opened by the chauffeur and out he stepped. It was an eye rubbing moment and I stood there paralysed from the shock of seeing him in the flesh. The legend, the genius of acting and the nicest person you will ever likely meet on and off the screen was there a mere twenty feet away from us. My dog like panting increased and I could feel a jolt of electricity surging through my body. It was Amitabh Bachchan. The guy I had seen on television around Dalj's house. The most famous Indian actor of all time walked past us and into the studios as the staff from within the complex fought off the myriad screaming fans and kept them at bay. He turned for a split second and winked at me. I was flabbergasted by it all. My head was in a spin. The legend winked at me. My life was complete and I would die a happy man.

Dalj smiled at me and Prity looked pleased for me too. It was the greatest tonic I could have asked for and it galvanised me to give it my best shot in today's auditions.

The smile on my face lasted for a few more hours after that moment and it made me want the same lifestyle of an actor that much more. This was despite continually catching the evil eye of Spiros throughout the morning.

Spiros and I were led to a room and both given scripts for the production of '*The Valati*' to read. The Valati translated as the foreigner and the part was written for a white guy like me or Spiros and the other dozen or so hopefuls that they had invited from other drama schools in the UK. I had been told that the basic understanding of Hindi was okay and that the part did not necessitate the actor speaking fluent Hindi or Punjabi anyway. I had learnt enough to get by from watching Bollywood films over the years ensconced in my bedroom and from the lessons that Dalj had given me as we grew up. So, I felt semi confident that I would be okay, besides which, I was aware that the winning actor would be given a crash course in any case and therefore it was a win-win situation.

During this session and while Spiros and I were left to our devices, I caught him checking me out. He appeared to be more interested in me than the script. Something was brewing and it was about to manifest itself when all of a sudden the door was opened and in came the other hopefuls. There were approximately ten guys of our age group and from various locations dotted around the UK. Most of them were stuck up individuals and no-one bothered to introduce themselves properly other than subtle nods of the head such was the supercilious air about them. At the end of the day this was a dog eat dog situation and I shouldn't have expected anything else. The guys all clutching scripts sat around the room and began pawing away at their lines. There was quite a lot to absorb in such a short space of time but I guess this was the ideal way in which to sort the wheat out from the chaff. I looked up at Spiros and he spat on the floor. I was threatening to rob this cretin of a future in the industry and the strain was obviously showing on his haggard face. He knew deep down that my acting skills had been meticulously praised over the years and I was staunch competition for him, a wily adversary and this thought gnawed away at his innards like a cancer.

'OKAY! Get up and follow me.' The voice boomed from the now open door. A jumped up upstart and lanky streak of gnats piss stood there twirling his handle bar moustache and chirping his instructions.

His curt approach already getting my back up instantly, despite being warned previously that the Bollywood industry was not for the faint hearted. I thought he was addressing a room full of flea bitten dogs rather than budding actors, but still followed him like the regular little Lassie that I was, trotting along behind the others with my tail wagging.

We walked into a proper film set with a stage and kitted out rooms. Once again, there was a feeding frenzy as a plethora of wannabes hung off of the arm of the director Jaspal, massaging his feet, fanning him and rushing off to get him cups of tea at the click of his fingers. It was unbelievable the amount of respect or fear depending upon your perspective that he commanded just by virtue of him looking at someone. Everyone but everyone danced to his tune, after all they had no choice as there were literally millions of other potential recruits hanging around the slum areas of Mumbai waiting for their opportunity to thrust their sandals through the door.

'Welcome my friends. I hope you have learnt you lines because that is the easy part let me tell you. Today and over the next few days I will be testing your ability to play the role of The Valati. If you don't think you can cut the mustard then I implore you to leave now.' He looked at me, 'But not you handsome,' he sniggered to himself before continuing to hold court. I found his behaviour quite erratic and unpredictable. It had dawned on me that he was not the kind of guy that I wanted to have following me in the shower after a football game clutching a bar of soap.

We all proceeded to take our positions on some seats that were provided and one by one we were asked to perform a set of lines from the script. It was all going swimmingly and all of this testing took the best part of three hours with Jaspal perched up high on his director's chair looking down at the peasants below him like an Indian Caesar.

All the while I could see Spiros making any excuse he could concoct to speak with him whilst the others performed and he waited his turn to step up to the mantle. His tongue was so far up the arse of Jaspal at one stage it made me cringe. I played it cool and studied the mistakes of the others and thus tried to consolidate my position in preparation for my turn.

'Spiros, you are next. Show me what you can do.' Jaspal lowered the clipboard he was holding and using to make comments on us hopefuls. Spiros looked as though he had a cup of water tipped over him. His face was a watery mess. The granules of sweat snaked around his forehead. He got up to chants of 'jaldi, jaldi (hurry up) from Jaspal and made his way to centre stage where he interacted with one of the stage team spouting lines from his script. It was my turn next and I could feel the butterflies in my stomach from the anxiety of the whole situation. This was it, it was make or break time and a blow out in my performance now would be disastrous. I wondered what Prity, Dalj and Pinto were doing outside as they waited for me. CLAP! CLAP! Jaspal cut Spiros to the quick and read out my name.

I started to walk to centre stage and saw Spiros sidle past me with a face like thunder.

I stood in my position and saw the stage member standing opposite me with a script held aloft. Jaspal was busy making some final notes from Spiros' audition and in doing so gave me a vital few final seconds to clear my throat and steel myself for the biggest moment of my life. Suddenly in the small gap between stage and back room I saw a misty figure floating there and giving me the thumbs up.

I focussed in on the figure. Who was it? Suddenly I found myself gasping for breath. It was dad. I could not believe my eyes. He floated for a moment or two smiling and showing me the good luck thumbs up signal. He was there in my time of need and he gave me the timely boost that I needed.

'SAM! SAM! I heard a faint noise as I wallowed in my bubble of contentment. Suddenly I was snapped out of my fervent cocoon when I noticed the stage hand jabbing at my chest with the rolled up script.

'We have not got all day,' they shrieked followed by several further chest poking jabs with the script.

I looked up at Jaspal and he did not look overly impressed by my stalling and apparent day dreaming. I thought about trying to convince him that I saw the ghost of my dad floating by at the back of the stage and that he was giving me the thumbs up but relented knowing full well that he would have had me arrested and sent off for drugs testing for hallucinogenic substances.

Then without any further interruptions from ghosts or otherwise I launched into my scene and delivered a decent account of my thespian talents. Mid way through as the stage hand and I exchanged lines like a couple of swash bucklers, I saw a figure at the back of the studio behind where the rest of the contestants were sitting. The shadowy figure lurched in and out of the shadows like a ninja and from their entire surreptitious behaviour looked as though they were up to some kind of malevolence. This distraction made me stumble a few lines much to the consternation of the stage hand and Jaspal, but I continued whilst trying to ignore what I had seen.

During my final exchange with my script partner, I clearly saw the shadowy figure as they began to walk hurriedly out of the studio. They stopped one last time and glared at me. It was Anil. What was he doing here? How was he supposed to get to me whilst I was auditioning? These thoughts shuttled around my mind. Jaspal clapped his hands and called a halt to the proceedings.

'Next time young man, you will need to concentrate on the task at hand rather than GOOFING AROUND IN MY BASTARD STUDIO! His saliva stained response disembowelled me where I stood. It was the death of a thousand cuts and the stage actually shook with his booming summing up of my first audition.

Suddenly I heard a rattling and clunking noise. I looked around desperately as did everyone else. The noise became louder.

'WATCH OUT!' screamed Jaspal. I looked up and momentarily froze in terror. An overhead light weighing at least ten kilograms had dislodged itself and was falling directly for my head. I gasped my last breath, bracing myself for when it hit me...I was dead for sure. My cat like reflexes had deserted me and I stood firm in readiness to meet my maker - Sardarji Griminder Reaperrjit. Like dad had said, I would meet my destiny in Bollywood and here it was. WHOOSH! SMASH! Down it crashed but not before I was expertly rugby tackled by the stage hand and whisked out of the way of certain death just as it shattered with a sickening thudding sound exactly where I had been standing. I screamed like a big girl's blouse and it took several moments of shaking from the stage hand to calm me down in the aftermath. I was a jangling bag of nerves.

I was quickly helped up to my feet and led off to a quiet room where I reflected on what had happened. It dawned on me that Anil had planned the 'accident' and had probably done it to show me that he could get to me no matter where I was. It had his signature all over it the slimy toad. I was in tatters and sucked up the warm mug of tea that had been provided to me. This had been a disastrous start and I was sure that my Bollywood dream was virtually over now. Why was Anil trying to kill me? It did not make any sense. If he was after the money, then killing me was not the way to get it. I was confused. I was certain that he had planned it to scare me.

I was joined by Spiros who did not say much but looked concerned for me judging by the mushy expression on his face. It seemed as though he was contemplating the thought that it could have been him underneath the light. The stage hand came back in the room and I thanked him profusely for saving my life. Even when they went to leave, I kept thanking them for being so heroic, metaphorically hanging on to their leg as they tried to escape my demented grasp while they tried to call the local mental asylum to collect me.

Outside the full story was regaled to the others and I sat in the back of the minibus with my head in Pinto's lap. She stroked my hair with her fingers and was quietly reciting a Punjabi hymn from the Guru Granth Sahib (the Sikh's holy book), it was therapeutic and sent me to sleep.

We made it back to the hotel without any further incident and in my sleepy haze heard Baldip talking about picking us up in a few hours to go to a party at Jaspal's house in the evening.

We all retired to our hotel rooms and rested for a few hours. The day had been stressful and I sat there licking my wounds and counting my lucky stars that I was still alive. It had been emotional.

Later that evening we arrived at a grandeur mansion on the outskirts of Mumbai. This was a palatial des res with panache, sophistication and pizzazz. I felt my mouth filling with drool at the mere sight of its imposing and baronial beauty. The wide reaching gardens stretching up and out into the backdrop of mountainous peaks merging with lip smacking splendour behind the veritable beauty that towered high above me. The ridge after ridge of spellbinding views stunningly situated and set amid rolling wooded grassland, with rustling palms swinging effortlessly and with aesthetic inspiration, it was a duvet of comforting serenity.

Jaspal greeted us with his spectacular pink shirt, the Rajput colour of hospitality he later told us, and his personal homage to the wonderful 'pink city' of Jaipur. Once inside I felt a visual assault on my senses yet again as I stepped into a world of sparkling chandeliers, marble floors, impressive architecture, rich wooded panelling, pristine custom designed furniture and an airy décor that perfectly portrayed a slice of Maharaj history that was mesmerising. One of his many servants served us some drinks before we started to relax a bit and enjoy the trays of culinary delights that he had laid on for the party.

There were quite a few guests at the party and as usual Spiros was following Jaspal around like a heat seeking missile. Wherever Jaspal was you could bet your knackers to a barn dance door that Spiros was sniffing around in close proximity. I spoke to Jaspal and he assured me that the incident with the light was a complete one off and nothing like that had ever happened before. He said that as a result all the lights were being over hauled and assessed for competency.

During my discussions with him I could see from the corner of my eye that Prity was being chatted up by several young frisky bucks but she seemed to be in control keeping them out of her personal zone.

Jaspal then called me to one side and whispered,' How badly do you want to make it in this line of work young man?'

It was a genuine question and I answered it honestly, 'It means the world to me sir. I would do anything to fulfil this life long dream.' I poured my heart out to him and knew that he held the key to my success so had no quibbles about being so candour.

'You would do anything? he asked.

'Well yeah. I want it really bad.'

'Hmm, well come in here a minute. I want to show you something.' He led me into a study on the ground floor and away from the hubbub of chatter from the other guests.

I walked into the dimly lit office behind Jaspal. I noticed we were alone, and for once I could not see Spiros' ugly mug poking out of the woodwork. I walked in and Jaspal closed the door behind me. I was certain that he was going to show me his photo collection or other such Holy Grail type secrets on how to make it big in the industry.

No sooner had I turned around, I heard the key being turned in the door. I looked at him, at the key in his hand and then at his face. He smirked naughtily and flashed me a Brokeback mountain glance that was deeply unsettling. Then in a move that would have made any Chippendale proud he whipped off his top and unbuckled his trousers in one foul swoop revealing his custard coloured pants. I stepped back to get away from him with fear coursing through my veins like an express train. It dawned on me that he was a crazy pervert as he stumbled towards me clearly aroused with his boner protruding rod like from his pants and seeking me out like a laser. I was not sure what to do and kept moving back slowly trying to evade the clutches of the one eyed monster, until I hit the desk at the back of the study and suddenly stifled any chance of a clean escape from the situation.

I saw him tapping out some white powder on to the back of his hand from one of his sovereign rings on his fingers and then with an almighty inhalation sucking the contents up into his nostrils. 'No, no, I am not that way inclined sir. Please stop!' I pleaded for the sexual maniac to leave me alone. I did not want to sleep my way to the top that was for sure. Worse still being buggered to make it to the top of the heap carried even less allure.

'Come on Sam. The first time is always the worse. After that you will be knocking on my door to get some. Trust me. I have been there.' His face turned into a scowl as he made a desperate lunge for me. Make no bones about it, if he had caught me at that moment I would have been sitting there for the next twenty minutes with an apple in my mouth, wearing a blonde wig and calling myself Suzy, not to mention waddling around with a sore arse for the next couple of weeks of added masala.

I managed to evade capture and grabbed the key that fell out of his grasp and on to the floor. I scooped it up and dashed for the door, putting it in and thankfully opening it to my freedom. With the door fully opened, I turned back and said, 'I am really sorry but this is not me. Do you still want me to turn up for the auditions or not?' I did not know what else to say.

I could see that Jaspal looked sheepishly embarrassed laying there half naked with traces of white powder scrambled on his chin and nose.

'Err, yes yes. This is our little secret isn't it Sam. Errr...see you at the auditions okay.' His voice was cracking and straining from the gravity of what had just occurred, it was some predicament and was career ending in his eyes.

I shook my head and walked out back into the land of sensibility and sanctity. I could see Spiros in the main meeting area searching frantically for his master. To be honest they were welcome to each other. I told Prity that I wanted to leave and summoned Baldip to take us home. After weathering the initial questions, I blamed it on some food that I had eaten and asked everyone to stop asking me any more probing questions as it was becoming like the Spanish Inquisition.

Spiros looked visibly upset when he was told that we were leaving and later took his anger out by shoulder barging past me as he went off to his room once we arrived back at the hotel.

That evening I told Prity and Dalj everything and as per usual she was my rock and Dalj was the perfect confidant. I arranged to meet up with Dalj early in the morning to spend a bit of man to man time with my best friend. He agreed and we set our alarm clocks for an early meet.

I took some pain killers and a decent shot of rum before bed and my lights were out before I could say 'you have been buggered.' I dreamt of an incident free day tomorrow but who was I kidding. The writing was already being inscribed on my tombstone and it was just a matter of time before the witching hour was upon me...

Chapter 11

The bionic Swami

Thursday 16th July – I met Dalj for breakfast downstairs in the garden of the hotel. I left Prity asleep and it appeared that we were the only two guys crazy enough to get up at such an ungodly hour. I checked my watch and it was seven fifteen am.

'Geezer. I think that we need some luck with all the bad stuff that has been happening to us. Don't you think?' He chomped on some toast as he spoke.

'I agree. What were you thinking?' I asked.

'I phoned mum and dad last night after you told me what had happened to you and asked them about that Swami that they saw some years ago. The guy who wrote out your teva and predicted your life.'

'You didn't tell them about, you know Jaspal trying to roger me did you?' I pleaded for the right answer to come from his lips.

'Nah don't be silly. I just told them about stuff like the lights and some people are out to get you. But guess what? They have given me an address for this Swami guy. I figure if we leave the others to do their stuff today, then we can go catch him and see what luck he can bring us. I think we can both do with some luck. What you saying mate?' Dalj's words made sense and his planning was timely as the next and final audition was not until tomorrow, (Friday 17th July), with the decision as to who had landed the part on Saturday 18th July. This gave us the day for our leisure, so I agreed, we finished off breakfast and I explained to Prity what I was doing and asked her to look after Pinto and perhaps show her the sights. I asked her to try and stay away from the pestiferous Spiros and she promised that she would avoid him like the bubonic plague.

Off we trotted to see Swami Durm Assa in his not so secret hideout in the middle of Karnala Forest approximately sixty kilometres from Mumbai. We hired a taxi for a return trip and were soon heading off on the road in search of good fortune and a little lady luck type magic to rejuvenate our flagging spirits.

An hour or so later we arrived at the entrance to Karnala Forest and National Park. We thanked the taxi driver and requested him to pick us up in a couple of hours. Dalj took out a small piece of paper from his pocket with a name and location details scrawled on it in biro. Notes he had hastily made when on the phone to his parents' last night.

We studied the location details for clues and followed the tree line dotted adjacent to the pathway. After several wrong turns and bouts of bickering and flying accusations of inferior map reading we found a clearing in amongst the trees deep in the bowels of the forest. Laying next to the clearing was a thundering waterfall cascading down into the swirling lake below. It was truly a sight to behold and I remained open jawed gaping at the magnificence of the scenery when I felt Dalj elbowing me in the ribs.

After the third elbow, I turned to him in annoyance and then to where he had sets his sights. There in the distance was a cross legged monk looking guy with a white sweeping beard dangling proudly to his feet. His hair tied up in a bun on his head and donning orange Hari Krishna style robes. He looked not a day younger than seventy but his nimble lotus position demonstrated his innate flexibility for all to see. We were alone with only the chirping of the birds in the trees offering any sound in this place of tranquillity. This was the haven of Swami Durm Assa and this is where for decades he had dedicated his life to provide followers and searchers of the truth with details of their destiny. I pinched myself to snap out of the over whelming inner serenity that was engulfing me. I felt like I could cruise on clouds, walk on water and make the sand dunes disappear. This was the aura of the place. We walked up towards this great man and quickly reached the foot of the waterfall, above us the legend sat in a peaceful trance like state.

Emotionless and stunningly quiet, he had not even heard us sneak up on him. I was impressed by it all. Then without any prior indication I heard the sound of 'You are the one that I want, ooh ooh oh,' being played somewhere. The tune continued for a few more seconds before stopping. I looked around at Dalj confused.

'Hello, yes I can book you in for a special appointment tomorrow evening.' We both looked up incredulous and it seemed that Swami had gone all twenty first century and was communicating on a mobile phone of all things. We shared the same look of disbelief as the Swami made good the arrangements with one of his punters finishing with,' Yes you can make the payments at www.swamidurmassa.com and if you book today you receive a special bonus of my book - 'I Did It My Way.'

He popped the phone back in his garments and caught us lurking with intent below him. He looked delighted, more customers and more business equated to more readies for the Swami dada.

'Welcome to my humble home my friends. You must be tired from your travels, please sit and have a drink with me before we start. The Swami negotiated a few treacherous looking steps and joined us at the foot of the fall. His embrace was warm and endearing, until I tried to suck in some fresh, clean oxygen and instead inhaled a whiff of his skunk like armpit. Never mind living next to a flaming water fall, this joker seemed like he hadn't had a splash of water on his body for eons.

Dalj also sported a pained expression and we both managed to wrestle ourselves free from his steely grip. He then disappeared in a cave and brought out some stools for us to sit on and then back he went again. We made ourselves comfortable as best we could. My nostrils were still stained with his pungent body odour and I picked and rubbed my nostrils many times to expunge the smell but to no avail. I sucked up eau de skunk with every breath I took.

Swami returned holding three steel glasses containing orange juice and offered them to us.

'You must be thirsty. Come, come drink up. This will give you dhanda's (todgers) of steel.'

He laughed and necked the entire contents, with some of the orange juice spilling down his chin and neck. I was feeling particularly parched after our journey and sunk the lot in one go, as did Dalj. The drink was strange, almost musty and with a bit of fire to it. The back of my throat began to burn and I felt sick. Hold on a minute, this was the strangest orange juice I had ever tasted.

Either that or the date had expired back in nineteen forty four or something. I looked at Dalj and he sat there looking quite satiated.

'What make of juice was that?' I asked Swami Durm Assa, hoping for an innocent explanation.

'Oh that is the first stage of purification. It is an old Indian tradition. Ask any grandma in your family,' he mumbled.

'Err, yeah but what is it Swami? What special ingredients do you use to make it so….well so rich, bitter and…?' I felt my stomach fighting the noxious substance that had been introduced to it.

'That is simple. It is my pee pee. This will put the spirit inside you quickly so that we can carry out our work smoothly.'

I immediately threw up and clutched my throat with both hands. Dalj ran head first into the lake and started drinking the water like a madman. I spat the remaining residue from my mouth on the floor, whilst simultaneously fiddling about with a black, wiry pube that was now lodged in-between my front teeth. I was not moved by the Swami's shoddy attempts at hospitality and wanted to make my feelings clear to him by grabbing him by the scruff of his wispy beard and rattling some sense into the rats maze he called his hairstyle. I stopped myself short of doing this when I noticed him chanting something over a small fire he had rustled up in-between our stools. He began to toss some leaves into the fire and motioned with his hands for us to sit down again. Dalj joined us completely soaked through to the bone from his earlier jump in the water.

The Swami stared at the fire, his face concentrated and through pursed lips started to hum. He clapped his hands furiously and then without a seconds notice quickly pulled out the burning leaves and tossed one on me and the other on Dalj. The freak show was now trying to burn us to a crisp as we both jumped off of the stools and dusted the burning leaves to the ground, jumping on them to put them out. I was mad by now, so mad that I was going to start throwing hands at this imposter. I looked at Dalj angrily, 'Are you telling me this village clown is the same imbecile who is responsible for judging my destiny. Are you kidding me or what?' Dalj felt the full brunt of my vehemence and hair drier type outburst.

The Swami sat there in a deep meditative state unmoved by the commotion he had already caused in such a short space of time.

'Yeah. I am one hundred per cent certain this is our man. I guess over the years he has gone a bit loopy.' Dalj tried to throw some much needed light on the guy's antics. He was a serious contender for Pinto's crown - that was a dead cert.

'This is a joke, a bloody shambles,' I shrieked at Dalj looking down at the hole in my shirt where the burning leaf had landed. It did not make sense. I was sure that I had unveiled an imposter and was ready to give him both barrels worth.

'Sit my sons, please listen I now have your future in my chakra. The vision and image is crystal clear. Sit, come.' He directed us back down on the stools, and reluctantly we both obeyed his command and sat down. This time I anxiously studied his hands for any dramatic manoeuvres involving burning objects being tossed in our direction.

I sat on my stool uneasily for the time.

'You are on the right path. You are here to make your dreams come true." He clapped his hands and chanted something.

'There is great danger for you Sam. You are a hunted man. There is lot's of money. I can see huge money, but I can see big heartache and pain for you.'

I studied the Swami for any form of jiggery pokery. Great danger, he was fucking right on that score, especially if he kept making me drink his piss and chuck burning bastard leaves on me. However, leaving all that to one side, what he was saying was an accurate portrayal of my life thus far. It was surreal but he was so right with what he had predicted.

'Be very careful, someone is going to get you and the fire will not tell me the outcome, but I see blood and danger, lots of blood and real terrible danger for you. Watch your back or it will be over.'

Oh well thanks for the edifying chat me old mate. That is just the tonic I needed to lift my spirits after the kind of week I have endured I thought. He was talking about Anil, Spiros or even Baldip snaring me. I searched for answers in my head. Maybe Jaspal wanted to teach me a lesson for insulting him in his own back yard. The Swami had given me problems and not solutions. I felt like I had reached my nadir and was full of low self esteem.

'If you make it past this Saturday then you will be very successful, but only if you make it past then. AAAAAAAGGGGGGGHHHHHHHHHH.'

The Swami screamed like a banshee before clapping his hands again and opening his eyes, full of smiles and the same goofy expression for which he was so loved.

I reeled back in surprise from his sudden paroxysm. Dalj looked equally startled too.

That was it, the ritual was complete and to my amazement I knew for a fact that I had never once mentioned my name or my situation to him, but yet he knew everything there was to know about me. He truly was a great Swami with this disturbingly magical aura that pervaded his every move.

'What about me?' squealed Dalj.

'Sorry but the Goddess of fire is sleeping now, so please come back later and I will tell you all about your destiny,' his response was sincere.

Dalj looked nervous and declined. He said that he was happy that my future was assessed and that although the warnings had been stark and revealing he was content for me.

We donated some money to the Swami for his prayers and headed back to the taxi for the ride back to the hotel. En route, I asked the taxi driver to make a detour to the bank so that I could speak with the manager. Dalj waited in the car and my appointment took half an hour or so. I had taken all the necessary forms of identification with me and I carefully secreted the contents of money that I withdrew in my pockets so as to not raise suspicion. I returned to the car and we chatted and speculated feverishly on the Swami's predictions in the taxi on the way back. At the hotel, I secretly deposited the money in the room and then touched base with Prity at the bar and met up with Pinto where I explained what had happened. A short while later I went to go to the toilet when Prity tugged my arm gently and whispered, 'I know you are a shrewd bunny, but just keep your guard up okay.'

I searched her eyes for answers. What was she getting at?

'You mean...' The words stuck in my throat.

'I am not saying anything babes, but just be careful…. Oh just ignore me, nothing, honestly it is nothing.'

'Hey.' She had confused me with this statement but she kept saying it was nothing and so we dropped the subject. I knew she was referring to Baldip and the beach transaction with Spiros. She was switched on enough to realise that the sharks were circling and had smelt blood in the water with regards to my inheritance money. I heeded her advice and took a few moments to compose myself in the toilet before rejoining the others.

We spent a good raucous evening drinking, laughing, and getting ripped to the tits on the swingeing amount of cocktails seducing us at the bar. Spiros and Baldip had also turned up during the festivities and joined in the frolicking. The evening truly felt like I was on holiday for the first time. I drank several cocktails, a couple of pints of Guinness and a few whisky chasers and revelled in the warm feeling skipping with great zest around my body. I was finally letting loose, kicking back and dancing with the spirit of '*Monsieur Nirvana*' and his esteemed relatives.

As the evening wore on, Prity and I decided to retire to our room where we would order some room service and watch some television. I felt like I was getting closer to my dream and just needed to get through the next few days unscathed. It would mean being one step ahead of my enemies.

We sat in our room and channel surfed for a few minutes. I left the task of ordering the food to Prity and I heard her negotiating on the phone with the catering people.

Whilst she was busy doing this I saw my mobile phone vibrating on the bed side table and reached across to retrieve it. The caller was unknown and I answered it right away for some reason, maybe it was the drink.

'Hey Sam. How you doing? It's Terry.' I almost fell off of the bed. The wily fox had tracked me down like the dirty dog I was. This untimely and deplorable intrusion had disaster plastered all over it as I felt my heart sinking to the pit of my stomach. What did he want with me? Why had he bothered tracking me down? I felt sickened and deadly scared…

Chapter 12

Hunger pangs

'I know you are in India. Where are you staying?' His voice was far too calm for what I remembered he was like. I did not answer and quickly put the phone down. I knew in my heart of hearts that this spelt imminent danger for me. Whatever happened to live and let live? Maybe this was the danger the Swami had foretold. I knew my goose was cooked, but from which direction remained a mystery.

Prity placed the phone receiver down at precisely the same time I terminated the shocking call from Terry.

The bomb was now ticking in more ways than one and the thought of Terry joining the rampaging mob out to maim or kill me was too debilitating for words. The manacles of oppression had taken hold of me and I knew that my dream trip would end up in someone losing their life. I could feel it in my waters, and to be honest if I were a betting man I would have thrown the house, the car keys and even my kidneys onto the betting table that I was the one due to meet a greasy end to this saga as Prity and Dalj were mere bystanders.

No sooner had I churned these worryingly nefarious thought around in my mind, the phone crackled into life once again. I knew it was Terry and let it ring and ring until it stopped.

'Who is that on the phone? Prity asked from across the room.

'Terry, the slimy bastard is in India and he is looking for me.' I responded grudgingly.

'Oh no, that is terrible. Does he know what hotel we are in?' she asked with a concerned look.

'I don't think so, but we just have to be careful, watch everyone and look around when we go out.'

Predictably, the phone continued to ring for the next half an hour with every call screened. Later it stopped much to my relief.

Prity told me that the catering staff had asked her to collect the food as their delivery waiter had phoned in sick that day and for the inconvenience they would discount our room service food accordingly, which I thought was a generous offer. I stood up to go and Prity insisted that she would go quickly and bring the food back within a few minutes and that I should rest due to the traumatic phone call I had received. I agreed and sat back on the bed and cogitated whilst my darling girlfriend winked at me and headed out of the door. I was a lucky guy having a cute looking girl like Prity on my side in this momentous battle that I was facing. I mean she was sexy, funny, hot and attractive – what more did I want?

Prity had been gone for about ten minutes and after getting up off the bed and shuffling patiently around the room I became concerned, especially after she had mentioned that she was only going to be a few minutes in getting the food. My heart started to bang like a tabla player on acid and within seconds, I found myself instinctively sprinting out of the room and down the corridor. I swept down the stairs like the wind blows, not even stopping to catch my breath or fully comprehend where I was actually heading towards.

Eventually after strenuous bounding down the multitude of stairs, I found myself bursting out into the reception area, huffing and puffing like an asthmatic. I gasped for air, hands on hips and wobbling about on unsteady feet. I looked up through water filled eyes and saw signs to the restaurant, and trotted off desperately towards that direction. I knew something was wrong, the air suddenly felt nauseating and I skilfully managed to suppress several vomit like convulsions whilst I foraged on. I had visions of seeing my gorgeous Prity lying there with her throat slit or strangled to death by the maniacs that were spreading through my life like a malignant cancer. I would never have forgiven myself for letting her get the food. Why did I let her go? I felt sick as I approached the final corridor leading to the kitchen and sitting behind the main restaurant.

I stepped forward with jelly legs, when suddenly in the distance I saw Prity walking through a set of doors from the kitchen holding a tray of food covered by silver foil. She had not seen me as she carried on away from me down the hallway, heading towards the restaurant carrying the tray delicately in both hands. I immediately felt the relief and accompanying endorphins racing around through my body. I was now ready for a champagne banquet such was the immense pleasure I derived from seeing Prity skipping majestically some distance from me. It was like the angels from heaven had descended and answered my every prayer. I felt gr…BANG! I stopped in my tracks. The tranquil moment was shattered when I saw a large grasping hand appear from a door and take a hold of her arm and violently pull her inside. I froze on the spot and realised regretfully that we had been mugged at the finishing line. It was a devastating finish to the dream. I urged my body forward to the room where my darling was being butchered, tentatively and like a broken man. I had been asphyxiated by Prity's love since the day I had seen her and now in her desperate time of need I stood by like a big wet lemon and watched her get picked apart by one of my enemies. You are right I was scared, I was nothing but a walking doodle. A gutless wonder, a flaming patsy. I heard a blood curdling scream and hysterical crying. My baby needed me.

I found myself standing outside the door struggling to pluck up the courage and set of kahoonas to enter and save her, fighting with my conscience to burst through the door like my hero Amitabh would do, guns blazing, fists flying and open a can of whup arse on the toe sucking cretin lurking within this chamber of horror. Instead, I suddenly found myself drawn into listening to the muffled voices within. The screaming had stopped and I heard the stern and menacing voice of Anil laying down the law to my girl.

'If I don't get my fucking money, then you will get it first you filthy whore. You feel me?'

This outburst was followed immediately by more muffled whimpering and pleading from Prity. What else could she have done in this quagmire of madness?

It seemed that the wolf had set up camp outside our door and Anil only had one putative purpose in his stinking life - to put the squeeze on decent people like us. I was aware that sometimes in life you have to take a few steps back to move forwards. It was all about judging the right time to react and right now, I found myself weighing up the risk and gravity factors of wading into the saloon bar like a gun slinging cowboy.

'Remember to tell lover boy that he has until Saturday or the curtain will fall for you both.' SLAP! I heard a crunching hand to cheek sound that made me wince along with the kind of yelp that sent a shiver down your spine. That was it I had heard enough, patsy or no patsy, scared or not, I was going over the trench and into the vault of terror to confront my tormentor once and for all. It was I had to do to ever be able to look at myself in the mirror again.

I looked around and the corridor remained lifeless as I firmly grasped the door knob with a sweaty and clammy mitt. This was it, I was going in. I felt the adrenaline shooting through my body like electricity, the pumping of my veins almost hydraulic and relentless. My eyes opened wide in anticipation as I saw the door knob being turned from inside. I felt my butt cheeks clench and realised I had to act fast. One wrong look, one Freudian slip now would end up with me being fished out of a lake somewhere. I could detect the hostility emanating from the other side of the door. Then it slowly opened, the gateway to Hell was unleashed on me. Too late, with a deft turn and footwork that Muhammad Ali would have been proud of in his heyday I found myself scarpering from the scene of the crime without so much as a hello or goodbye. There was no legislating for my behaviour, I was running purely on instinct and it was a culmination of being abused and victimised by everyone for years that had caused me to act in such a deplorably sheepish manner.

I was ashamed and cowered in an adjacent room peeking through the slight gap in the door that I had opened ever so slightly. You would have heard of He-Man and the power of Greyskull. In my case it was like the power of tosser and I felt sick to the pit of my gutless stomach. I continued peeping through the crack in the door trying to catch a glimpse of my nemesis. I was not disappointed when he walked out, once again dragging her helpless frame from within and thrusting her against the wall opposite the room. The thud reverberated through to where I was cowering some feet away in this darkened linen room. Anil uttered some final threats before walking past my door leaving Prity a shaking and crumpled mess further down the hall. He strode past the door like a conquering hero having served a birthday cake of hurt to my sweetheart. All of a sudden he stopped and slowly turned his head to look at the crack in the door where like any good cartoon all you could see were the whites of my eyes shining in the darkness, peering back at him. He possessed the kind of look that made you want to fill your nappy, a look that said that he could take your soul from you at any given moment. The blood in my veins froze, had he seen me? Years of servitude had lent itself to this situation where I was shamelessly hiding behind a door whilst all hell was breaking out around me. I resigned myself to the beating that was about to ensue and stood back from the door. It was over and I was running on empty. I stared back at the faint glimmer of light that shone through the door into the darkness of my soon to be tomb. My back pressed up against a heavily stacked linen shelf. I held my breath and then closed my eyes. I hated surprises and if he wanted to get me then I didn't want to see it coming that was for sure. I waited and waited. I felt myself licking my parched lips with my dry tongue, my throat dryer than the most baron of deserts.

Nothing, just stony silence both in and out of the room. I slowly opened the door and poked my head up and over the parapet. The corridor was empty and even Prity had disappeared. I puffed out my cheeks in sheer relief. Without wasting another second, I dragged myself back down the corridor and up to my room, all the time, looking nervously at every nook and cranny of the hotel, just to be sure. Eventually I made it to the room and noticed that the door was ajar. I heard rustling inside and felt uneasy. Anil had broken into my room and was laying in wait for me. I quickly scanned the corridor, I was not sure what I was looking for in particular but knew that if I saw it I would know. My hands began to shake as they did down in the kitchen hallway, my body a simmering hotbed of anxiety. I could see the headlines now, the front page news, *'Apprentice actor slain in his own hotel room. His body parts dismembered by a rusty hacksaw as killer leaves his calling card.'*

Then I saw it, a vase in the distance. I raced over to it tipping the flowers and water to the floor and walked back purposefully to the room. This was it, no more Mr nice guy. I was going to get my respect, my revenge, and my life back once and for all. I tried to control my Darth Vader type breathing and with that, I looked down at the vase and up at the door. I had just about had enough of being the victim in life.

What I wanted to do was burst through the walls on my motorbike or horse and make a grandeur entrance as they do in the Bollywood films but there wasn't time, besides which it would have been a logistical nightmare trying to get a horse up the stairs of the hotel. The rustling grew louder and more sinister and I suddenly and violently kicked the door open and burst through wielding the vase above my head, screaming like a demented banshee – YAAAAAAAAHHHHHHHHH. I looked up and realised that this was a bad, bad mistake, but it was too late…

Chapter 13

Reflective fortitude

It was a bad mistake all right and certainly too late for me to stop myself looking like the village idiot as my screams died down. I stood there holding a vase above my head and saw Prity dutifully rustling the silver foil off of the tray and pouring our meals out on to our plates. My screaming and entrance making her jump out of her skin in the process. She looked at my wild eyed and unhinged look before breathing a sigh of relief. It was one of those moments when I had wished the ground would open and swallow me up with it.

'What are you doing?' she asked quizzically. I sensed her fingers itching towards the telephone for the men in white coats to come and scoop me up with a dog catcher net.

This was the crucial moment where I had to decide if I should confess to having seen her turmoil moments before or try and bluff my way out and prevent exposing myself as a toothless hick.

I went for the weasels approach, 'How come you took so long with the food?'

'Err, it wasn't ready babes. Erm, but it is here now, come and eat before it gets cold.'

It was patently obvious that she was shielding me from the ordeal she had endured. It was just her nature to think of others before herself and to be frank with you I kind of loved that about her.

I turned around and noticed that Dalj had appeared in the doorway, along with Pinto and even Spiros amongst other hotel guests from our corridor all rubber necking like ghouls to see what the commotion was all about. They had heard the scream and kicking of the door.

Dalj had a concerned look on his face, 'What the hell is happening dude?' he asked.

'Oh no nothing geezer, I just went to look for Prity and when I got back I saw the door open and thought that we had burglars or something, that is all.' I spun him a line and looked over at Prity's reaction. She was equally taken in with my story. Job done I mused. I replaced the vase outside whilst the guests retired back to their rooms noticeably aggrieved that they had not seen the sought after excitement that they had hoped for in the form of a violent domestic incident, the parasitic bastards. Spiros cast a sinister glare before skulking off back to his lair. Dalj and Pinto returned to their rooms and I locked myself in the toilet for a bit whilst I grappled with my thoughts. After pebble dashing the toilet with yesterday's food I sat on the bed with Prity devouring the food like a good one.

I searched her face for clues. I guess I did not have to be Sherlock Holmes to assess what had happened as I had seen it first hand, but was a little perturbed why she was not confessing her ordeal to me. It was worrying and we both sat there in silence chomping away at our dinner. The kind of silence where I could hear every irritating crunch, every grinding of roti slipping down her gullet and every slurp of tea. All throughout we both remained tight lipped about what had happened. My yearning to reach out and hug her was over whelming and I knew that she was putting on this brave face to protect me from the news that she knew I feared.

We finished our food and kicked back on the bed channel surfing through the various programmes, mostly in Hindi on the TV set nestled on the table at the foot of the bed. She lay there with her head in my chest and twirled her finger through the button holes in my shirt. This was a nice moment and a far cry away from the mayhem of what had occurred earlier.

'Do you think we should go to the police? asked Prity.

I played devils advocate, 'What for babes? We just need to get Saturday out of the way and it will all be okay, right.' I was a good actor, that was for sure.

'I am just thinking that things may get out of control with that Anil guy and stuff, err, would it not be good to at least make the police aware of him and what he can do?' her voice was plastered with doubt and dejection.

I composed my response knowing full well that her jousting questions were the sure fire signs of a one in a million girlfriend and that she would rather suffer herself than to expose me to this fate.

'Like I said before, I will give that arsehole the money and then we can just get on with our lives. I will hope to make that money back as an actor if I make it and then at least we will have got them all off of our backs once and for all.'

Prity stared back at me with her big, beautiful eyes, they were swimming in water with little trickles beginning to slowly snake their way down her cheeks. She even cried like an angel. I smiled reassuringly and gave her an anaconda type hug whilst kissing her on the forehead. Tomorrow would be one further step towards my goal and as long as I could outfox the hordes of cronies out to lynch me, I knew I would be the one smiling when the dust settled.

'You will come to no harm my darling. I promise you. I will be here to protect you from everyone.' I talked a good fight and even thought about fighting like a Bollywood hero, but in recent years felt the fight had been sucked out of me from incident after incident. In life you either choose to be a worker ant or a queen bee and after today's tumultuous incident that I had witnessed I was understanding that I wanted to become the latter. I was ready to fight back now. This was the time of reckoning and I was more than ready to slug it out with my enemies. This was a moment of clarity, forget the rock and roll music, forget the John Wayne swagger, I was primed and raring to get what I wanted. At this moment, I felt like I could float on water as the emotions built up inside me. Thoughts such as these whirred around in my head for an hour or so, my dreamy triumphalism edifying me to my core.

I had visualisations of me unleashing the dogs of war on all the haters, and other such stimulating thoughts sending me off into the land of deep slumber. Prity and I lay there entwined as one and snugly away with the fairies. I knew my Winston Churchill type thoughts were nourishing for my soul but the reality knocking on the door reminded me that to extricate myself from this awful mess would not be so easy. It would mean coughing up the green to Anil, moving out from Terry and Myleene's house and setting up with Prity somewhere, avoiding the clutches of Spiros and after trying to secure this one acting contract with the director Jaspal Verma, moving on to work with other successful directors and projects. This was the blueprint and formal roadmap to success imprinted in the depths of my grey matter, but despite this cradled haven of peace and serenity I found myself in with my beau, I knew that death lurched nearby and I was truly in dire straits no matter how much I reached down and felt I had a pair. Monsieur's doom and gloom were coming to my party whether I liked it or not and for now I rested my body in commencement for the carnage of the following day.

Chapter 14

Smokescreen

Friday 17th July – One more day to go until the question of my destiny was answered. I was content that we had broken the back of the process thus far and woke to the sound of knocking on my door. I rubbed my eyes and looked at the time – eight a.m. on the nose. Who was this punctual irritant banging outside? I slithered out of the duvet and opened the door to be confronted by Baldip in all his grisly glory. He looked bright eyed and bushy tailed and smelling like he had been bathing all morning in a tub of Kouros aftershave.

'Morning sir.' he yelped before excitedly storming past me with his briefcase swinging by his side.

'Err, do you want us to meet you in the reception? I asked imploringly. The last thing I wanted was to have Baldip sniffing around when my girl was getting ready, I mean that was just not right.

He smiled and uttered, 'See you in the restaurant garden for breakfast, no rush, we have some time to discuss progress before the final audition today.' With that he took his charged up body out of my room, almost clicking his heels as he trotted off. It was obvious that he had got some that morning gauging his buoyant demeanour.

A short while later Prity and I joined the motley crew downstairs in the garden area of the restaurant for some much needed fuel to kick start our day. They say that breakfast means exactly that, to break your nightly fast by virtue of the fact that your body has been starved of essential nutrients throughout the twilight hours and to get up and have a hearty meal in the morning was like putting petrol in your car. Well it made sense to me as bits of bacon and egg dribbled down my mouth.

Pinto tucked into her scrambled eggs with great rapacity, even eating her toast with two hands, like you would hold a sandwich in her innocence. Dalj looked well groomed and a sure fire contender for having the best nights kip from all of us. Spiros was his usual mundane grunting self and slurped his tea from the other side of the table while constantly shoulder surfing. A term used when someone is listening to the conversation but flitting his eyes over the shoulders of the people speaking with him so as to catch the eye of someone more important or interesting. Prity was quiet this morning and nibbled on her toast without quibble. Baldip lifted all of our flagging spirits regaling us with stories from the industry despite Spiros shoulder surfing all the way through. Dalj meanwhile was quite chatty and managed to drag me from my gloomy frame of mind. After a short while and with the contents of the mornings breakfast nestled firmly in our stomachs the conversation became more animated and bubbly, with everyone chipping in with their two pennies worth of stupefying facts and stories.

I noticed Baldip answering his mobile several times during the course of this early part of the morning. He would answer it and then excuse himself from the table before engaging in deeper conversation with the caller over the other side of the restaurant. I also noticed that he was indeed looking flustered each and every time he done this. Prity who put the 'R' in razor sharp had picked up on his frequent mobile interruptions and turned to me and whispered, 'There, I told you to watch out for him didn't I. Who is he talking to on the phone so many times?' she looked visibly distressed by his actions. I could see that Dalj had also honed in on our conversation and he cast me a quizzical look as if to ask if everything was okay.

I nodded my head and alleviated his worries temporarily. It was not the time and place but I would fill him in after regarding Prity's concerns, after all he was one of my few but staunchest confidants.

Baldip returned looking red faced and flustered and sat back down.

'Who was that? Prity went straight for the jugular. I sat there squirming with the taste of egg swirling in my mouth and praying that we did not unearth some dark and duplicitous secret so early in the day.

'Oh, just some business I am taking care of.' Baldip looked nervous and like a rabbit in the headlights. The sweat dripping off of his forehead like a tap.

'You are sweating big man, what's the deal?' Spiros chipped in cunningly and with no quarter spared in his pursuit to illicit the truth out of our aide.

'Yeah it is a hot day you see. Come let's go.' He motioned for the waiter to come over and settled the bill for us. Meanwhile I went to the toilet as did one or two of the others.

When I returned everyone was heading off towards the minibus when Prity held me back my arm and said,

'I am even more convinced that he is not genuine now. I don't know why but I don't trust him as far as I can throw him.' Prity's face scrunched up looking as though she was chewing a wasp.

'He is after your money. I am telling you he has contacts in the banks, he will get your account numbers and you will end up with nothing. Trust me I have good intuition, he is a wrong un.'

She was convincing that was for sure. In summing up her case at the crown court she had Baldip ready to be hung, drawn and quartered for looking a bit shady. It was apparent that his smokescreen was not working on her and I tried my best to appease her. I had to focus on what was important at this time, securing my acting contract with this new movie. It took me several moments but I had successfully managed to convince her to call off the blood hounds just for a while longer. She agreed but could not help cutting her eyes at Baldip whenever she had an opportune moment. Her discontent was tangible and like a volcano waiting to erupt.

In the minibus on the way to the film studio Spiros sought the opportunity to crank the stereo up so that he could listen to someone who it appeared was slowly strangling a cat with piano wire and was attempting to entertain us with their best vocals on the local Hindi radio channel. The sound blared out at an indecipherable level assaulting our ears in the process. Why would he do that to us? This trip was taking its toll on me and I was missing 'Blighty' with a vengeance by now.

Dalj meanwhile turned to me and under the cloak of the cat strangulation music whispered, 'Look, I know what you and Prity were talking about and if you want my opinion I am totally down with what she is saying.'

I stared at him trying to comprehend his thought process.

'Yeah I think that worm is after your money mate. Just look at the way he looks at you. Remember what he said when we met him about him being connected in this industry. Don't you think he knows people in the banks and all that? I reckon you would be best to avoid him if you get what I mean.'

'You serious?' I asked seeking absolute confirmation of my friends judgement.

'As serious as tooth decay my friend. Get rid of that leech now or god help me I will do it for you.'

His qualities as a mate were noble and admirable and it was clear that he was being disarmingly open about his feelings. It also meant that he had spoken to Prity about his suspicions which in itself was not a bad thing.

His words echoed what Prity had said to me and it was the final confirmation that I had needed. I smiled knowingly and knew what I had to do. Remember when I said that I was a good actor, well I was stepping up for a Bafta award now. I smirked to myself for the rest of the journey whilst sizing up some of the things that Baldip had already done and displayed in the short time that I had known him. The beach incident where he was seen speaking to Spiros, Anil magically appearing on the scene, the clandestine calls at every opportunity, the detected glances towards Spiros, the knowing looks that I had observed with Jaspal and…the call from Terry trying to track me down. It all meant one thing and manifested itself to one conclusion - he was in cahoots with someone and he was out to scupper any chances I pined for to leave the country with my life or money.

They say knowledge is power and confidence is built from being one step ahead. I felt that I had moved on to a different time zone let alone mere steps and kept this thought close to me whilst Baldip thankfully killed the music and steered the minibus into the car park outside the Bollywood Film City Studio.

Inside I knew what I had to do to avoid being dragged down to my knees by this newly added nemesis to the melting pot. Dad was right when he told me in physical presence and in spirit to always be on my guard, and boy did I have to watch my step with a few people. I was being sold like a run away slave as fear and danger surreptitiously stalked me.

We alighted the minibus and headed off into the studio. The usual plethora of dancers, hanger on's, cast and crew members all milled around resembling a normal day at a busy London underground station. Everyone was in their own little world and were like little workaholic beaver's knuckling down in their respective jobs.

I saw Prity asking Baldip if she could use his phone and he obliged. Meanwhile I was distracted by Jaspal who turned up in a purple suit with large protruding white collars poking out from the lapels. The forest that was his chest hair was an invitation for a lit match if ever there was one. He strutted around in his purple suit like the human dinosaur that he was, aptly nicknamed Blarney by us - the king of bullshit - rather than Barney the purple dinosaur. Dalj and I continued stifling our sniggers like a couple of naughty school children throughout the morning, with occasional elbow nudges in the ribs making us squeal like wounded hippos.

Later that day after we had been put through our paces once again, Prity called me over to one corner of the studio. I could sense that it was something urgent and excused myself to see what had happened.

When I reached her she looked shaken and deeply distressed. What had happened? I placed my hand on her shoulder and asked, 'Darling what's happened? Has someone said something to you?' I could feel my blood boiling and I had got to the point where I would defend my girl religiously should anyone try and take advantage of her. I was ready to rumble with the guy who had upset her on this occasion, to be frank I pitied the fool.

She handed me a mobile phone with a trembling hand. It was Baldip's mobile phone.

'Babe I am sorry but I had to confirm my suspicions, I am so sorry.'

I took hold of it and slowly looked down at the screen. My heart jumped in my mouth. It was a phone number saved in the phone memory. It was Anil's number. He had been caught with his hand well and truly in the cookie jar. His days of being a moustache twirling baddie had come to an end.

Prity looked devastated for me, I could tell that by the transparency plastered over her face.

She flicked a few more buttons and showed me another number and this time I felt another crushing blow to my gut. It was the phone number of Terry, also stored neatly into the phone memory. I gripped the phone tightly almost crushing it with a wave of freakish strength that had suddenly began to course through my volcanic like body. Why was he doing this to me? I did not understand.

It was true when I had heard the rumours about many Bollywood agents being corrupt and how Asian businessmen were motivated solely with making a quick buck out of any unsuspecting fool who was ready to part with their hard earned money. I felt like curling up in a ball on the floor and licking my own skin like a dying cat. What strength did I have left? I was emaciated, deceived and now the heavy weight champion of suckers. I handed the phone back to Prity and she lunged forward and hugged me so tight I was sure she was trying to squeeze the turtle head out of arse that had just appeared in this surreal moment of anguish. I felt my lungs collapsing as she held on for dear life, like she was on some kind of bucking bronco.

She then let go as my cheeks were starting to turn blue and kissed me full on the lips before lifting my soul from the cobbled gloom of the studio floor.

'You have to do what you have to do when we go back to the hotel, okay!'

Her words were as lucid as the treachery from Baldip was palpable. I knew exactly what I had to do and how he was going to pay for his Judas type back stabbing.

Prity rubbed her hand up one of my arms and then walked back and out of the studio. I saw her innocently hand the phone back to Baldip as he talked to some actors through the window and gritted my teeth before returning to my acting audition with Spiros. Despite wanting to use the toilet I was aware that any faux pas now would end in total unmitigated disaster for me so kept the turtle at bay for the next hour or so before being allowed to nip to the toilet for the ceremonial head squeeze in trap one.

I sat there and looked wistfully at the scrawling on the wall. When suddenly, one such scrawling popped out at me - it read;

'Success awaits you, but it will probably arrive after much sacrifice!

Be aware of Karma and balance your desire with the thought of being happy!

Have you got what it takes to be the next 'Paisa Vasool?' (Meaning money's worth for Hindi film viewers).

If you are reading this then I have shagged your sister, ha ha you mother fucking fart sniffer I got you!!!

Despite the last entry being subsequently inserted by some pestiferous individual, I was dumbfounded.

The only thought shuttling through my mind was the fact that it appeared that fucking Confucius had been defecating in this same stinking hell hole shitter as me, after all who else could have composed such a pearl of wisdom whilst knocking one or two out?

After I had finished I cleaned up and started to wash my hands in the basin, catching a glimpse of my reflection in the mirror. It was true I looked like a bag of wallowing self pity. Suddenly something moved quickly behind me, I turned, but was met with emptiness, just dozens of brooding cubicles staring right back at me. I then heard a creaking noise and slowly inched forward to investigate what this shadow was.

I pushed open the first cubicle and there was nothing, the second, nothing, the third – BANG! I fell back on the floor. I looked up expecting the flash of a gun or steel of the knife blade thrusting in and out of my throat. I was in utter shock and looked up helplessly, this was the moment where I would meet my grisly end, it had been written in my 'teva.' Suddenly, from out of the cubicle the ghost of my father appeared.

'Hello son.' he chirped.

'Dad, what the hell are you doing? Will you stop creeping up on me like that you will give me a heart attack or something. I clutched my heart as I stood to my feet, resting on the wash basin.

Dad laughed and said, 'Heed the warnings you have been given and remember follow your dreams with great fervency.'

'I will, but can't you just tell me what is going on. Surely you have got the best vantage point being up in the sky looking down on everyone. Just listen in a few conversations for me and fill me in, it will make my job easier you know.' I was being half facetious.

'This is against the rules. Don't worry son I am here for you. Just don't give up your passion and you will be a resounding success.' With that he disappeared in a puff of smoke.

'Next time send me an invite and how is mum?' I shouted looking up to the ceiling. I missed him sorely and wished that he could have been around in my formative years. It would have made all the difference. I wiped away a couple of stray tears that flowed carefree down my cheeks and resolved myself for the last day and a half of battling that I was inevitably up against. It was going to end in tears for someone and my destiny was going to be decided on the toss of a coin for all intents and purposes. I walked out of the toilet a man full of the world's worries and with a whole zoo full of monkeys on his shoulders. What was next for me, I had no idea…

Chapter 15

Bloodbath at the 'Mumbai Coral'

The final auditions were drawing to a close and we had been vigorously tested through a series of relentless tasks from a whip cracking Jaspal and his crew of sadistic buffoons. I am certain that Jaspal went out of his way to make life a living hell for me when he dished out his orders for the auditions. Everything I did, every scene I tried to act was lambasted. I was becoming more disillusioned by the second and it was his way of seeking retribution from that day at his house when I had rebuffed his advances. He owned my destiny in the palm of his perverted hand and I was being put through the paces. The day was heavy and burdensome, with every fibre in my body urging me to go to sleep in some deserted corner of the studio, to close my eyes and let the pain vanquish as if by magic.

I caught Prity's eyes a couple of times during the torment whilst she was eating a snack and I could see from her look that she felt my pain. I caught Dalj studying the proceedings closely and on the other hand stopping Pinto from playing with the props by the side of the stage and seating area.

I wondered what Prity saw in me? I mean without sounding my own trumpet I knew that I was quite a good looking chap and I had a well grounded and pleasant personality but boy did I come with my issues. I had more baggage than an airport carousel, but she loved me nevertheless, the hallmark of a decent girl. A short while later and Jaspal stood centre stage clapping his hands several times and marking the end of my misery. A victorious Spiros clapped and led the sycophantic adulation for the chance to audition at the studios, with the other people or should I say '*sheeple*' following suit and clapping like demented seals.

I refrained and instead hopped off the stage with just enough time to hear Jaspal stating that the final results would be held tomorrow morning and for us to all be in attendance. I knew my journey had come to an end and felt like blubbing like a big fat girls blouse, I had come all this way for what reason? To be shamed and humiliated in such a denigrating fashion. What because I didn't sleep with the director I thought painfully? It was not fair, but then again who said life was? Just look what demons I had endured already in such a short life. This was one more of those look how far I got stories. I trudged off a broken man.

'Hey!' a voice appeared behind me.

I turned to see Spiros standing there, grinning at my patent plight. Something felt engineered here but I could not put my finger on it.

'May the best man win, okay!' he chirped thrusting his hand out for a hand shake. I felt repulsed and cheated but as a gentleman extended my hand and shook it lightly. As I did he pulled me in close to him so that I could feel his hot breath on my cheek and snarled, 'I always knew I was better than you, always!' He let go and I reeled backwards from the force. I had grabbed the hand of the wolf and he was as sinister and malevolent as they came.

We set off once again in the minibus and on the way back I kept getting nudges from Dalj to sort the situation with Baldip out. He wanted me to confront him about the mobile phone. Prity remained quiet and stared out of the window watching the Mumbai world go past. She was tired and I could see her eyes becoming heavier and heavier before she slipped into nap land, getting some much needed siesta time. She had fallen victim to the classic sure fire tenets that make you sleepy, the first one being the fact that everyone no matter who you are all suffer from tiredness in the afternoon, usually around three o clock but varying depending on when you wake up. This mid afternoon crash or burn out is caused by nature's way of designing humans so that we sleep in the afternoon like we did when we were kids. It is also due to the fact that our blood sugar drops slightly lower than normal at this time. This was the prime reason why the Spanish in particular close their shops in the afternoon so that people can have that much needed siesta and recharge their batteries. The second reason she drifted off was because she had been snacking earlier. When you do this, the blood always concentrates on the stomach when you have eaten to help you digest the food, it therefore goes away from the brain and other areas inducing sleep. Well enough of the biology lesson, I am in the shit here.

I tapped Baldip on the shoulder and asked him to pull over in a local service station so that I could get some food and also talk with him. He winked at me through the rear view mirror and seconds later duly obliged by pulling into a local eatery and roadside service station. He had no idea of the slither of well armed questions that we had rolled up our sleeves and ready to bombard him with in the next few minutes of Hell.

We got out of the vehicle when without any prior warning Dalj forcefully took hold of Baldip and pushed him roughly against the side of the van screaming, 'What are you after then you parasite? Come on talk to me you haramzada.' Baldip looked visibly shaken and started to stutter.

'Ahh, see he is stuttering, the truth is sticking in his throat. I knew this fucker was trouble the moment I saw him.' Dalj seemed proud of his detective work.

I mean how did Dalj know he was trouble the moment he saw him? Did he have spidy sense? Sixth sense? What the fuck!

Dalj continued to rattle Baldip so hard that the change began to jingle and jangle out of his pockets on to the dusty road. Then in a scene that will haunt me forever there was an avalanche of kids running and screaming heading towards us like their little sandaled lives depended upon it. They had been circling like predators and now they had seized the moment they were relishing – money up for grabs. The fact that there was change on the ground was five Christmases rolled into one. They descended on us on ropes, by parachute, torpedo, and even rising from the earth just to get the twenty or so rupees in loose change that Dalj had shook out of the beleaguered Baldip.

'Stop it! Stop it will you! He will tell you his name is Elvis Presley the more you intimidate him, what's the matter with you Dalj?' I freed Baldip from Dalj's grip more or less using a crowbar such was his intent. I then led him into the restaurant and asked Dalj to wake Prity up and bring them all inside so that we could get some snacks after the rigours of the day.

The Indian sanitation left a lot to be desired. I has stepped over dog faeces to enter the restaurant and almost vomited Exorcist style at the humming aroma that the entrance to the gents was wafting in to the main area, or was that the kitchen? I could not tell either way. I noticed that there were a pack of dogs fighting over scraps in the car park and occasionally entering the restaurant to see if they could mug any greenhorn tourists as they sat at the tables risking their own lives as they did so. Any one of the dogs would have been suitable for the lead role in the Cujo film, with there flaky flea bitten skin and accompanying diseased breath panting over the diners as we walked in.

We picked a table, sat down and ordered some light snacks with Baldip looking understandably pale faced. I kept Dalj on a tight leash and away from striking distance and saw Prity nodding her head subtly as though giving me approval for the line of questioning that was about to ensue.

'Okay now tell me the truth, just yes or no. Have you been in touch with Anil or Terry?' I threw the question out there and studied his facial expressions to evaluate the veracity of the response that I knew would be forthcoming.

'Who is Anil and who is Terry bhai saab?' He answered softly and with trepidation. His lip was beginning to quiver, the obvious sign of a snake out of his depth. He had been caught with the smoking gun and no amount of denying his sudden exposure was going to emancipate him from the crucifixion that loomed ominously. Spiros looked on with fascination as to what was happening, whilst Dalj growled at this meek retort from Baldip.

'The numbers were found in your phone. Why have you phoned them?' I asked again.

BANG! Behind me, I heard a glass smashing to the floor and saw a group of Indian Hells Angel types come crashing through the doors, marking their entrance in a flamboyant and reckless manner. There were four young hoodies and they all appeared drunk and began to terrorise some of the guests within.

I turned back and asked again, 'Look what is going on mate? What do you want?'

Baldip lowered his head, he was shamed and remained like that for the next few minutes as a furnace of questions and accusations were fired at him from every conceivable angle and on virtually every topic under the sun. It was like being on a quiz show in the land of amphetamine speed such was the voracity and pace of questions. Baldip stone-walled all of us, and the guilt covered his disingenuous carcass like an overcoat. He was as guilty as charged and had all the attributes of a spineless blob, with traitor indelibly etched across the expression of guilt on his forehead. Why had he seen fit to drive a stake through the heart of my ambition, why?

Right at that moment I held Dalj back as he leapt up from his seat and tried to grab a hold of him over the table. He had seen too many Bollywood movies and was trying to finish the scene with a bang, preferably on the nose of Baldip. I stopped him and cajoled him back into his seat. Spiros laughed and shook his head, 'Now this is what I call entertainment. What the hell is going on?'

Dalj quickly filled him on what had been going. I was dubious about how much information that Dalj was going to divulge as I did not know exactly what relationship that Spiros also had with Baldip, but I allowed him to sing like a canary for this moment.

'Right that is it then, you had better go. I never want to see you again, you understand!'

I poked Baldip in the chest. This jolted him back to life and he moved his eyes across the floor like an Action Man figurine.

'We will make our own way back in a taxi, now get out of my life!' I shouted.

Baldip got up and slowly mooched out of the restaurant, embarrassed and exposed as the back stabber he was. Prity muttered an English profanity under her breath whilst Dalj shouted some Punjabi expletives towards his direction. Even Pinto called him 'a bhanchod' (a sister fucker) as he left for the last time. He turned back just once and looked at me for confirmation that his fate was sealed. I nodded my head and rubber stamped his expulsion from our lives, and at that moment like a puff of smoke, he was gone forever.

We sat there and discussed what had happened. In all fairness even Spiros looked miffed about what he had heard about the shenanigans of the past few days events. He was stunned to hear about the phone numbers in Baldip's phone and made a hypocritical point of stating that this industry had no room for duplicitous liars like him. I almost choked on my hot dog when he said that as we all continued to chat.

I then heard a wolf whistle, followed by another one. It was the group of guys who had come in before. They had successfully managed to empty the restaurant of all other people with our group being the only ones left and they had now honed in and locked their horns on us.

'Oi, kidda sweetie?' One of the trouble makers yelled. The waiters and other staff knew that trouble was brewing and like a Western they all cowered beneath the counter leaving us to our own devices to fend the trouble makers off.

'Not hearing me properly you saali, I said kidda sweetie?' the gang leader, a six foot five inches tall, stubbly and spotty oink shuffled over to our table like Herman Munster and looked directly at Prity and no-one else. She looked terrified and searched my face for an answer to this SOS situation that had cropped up from nowhere. The thug would have made a good Bond villain and was just missing the gold teeth.

I knew that when or if ever returned home that I would be searching for a bastard rabbit's foot as yet another tumour developed in my plans. Everywhere I seemed to go there was violence, arguments or hostilities there in heaps.

I took one more bite of my hot dog and placed the remainder neatly back on my plate. I looked across at Dalj and then at Spiros and they looked scared and rightly so remained tight lipped hoping that the drunkard would eventually get tired and leave us alone. I on the other hand had just about had enough belly aching, running scared and pussy footing rubbish to last me a lifetime and had already made my mind up to stop this nonsense from exacerbating any further. Lurch was being cheered on from his *'girlfriends'* sitting away from us at the other table and the single most annoying thing about the incident was that the thug towering above us to my side never once looked at me or gave me the time of day. He obviously felt that I posed an insignificant threat to him, either that or he was about to eat my liver for his dinner. I stood up just as the thug was about to metaphorically club Prity on the head, and drag her into his cave.

'Can I help you? I asked the man mountain.

'GRRRRR!' was the articulated response that I got back.

I went to speak again when I felt the crushing strength that this brute possessed as he flung me across the adjacent tables with such force I could feel my teeth rattling. I stood up and felt a trickle of blood seeping out of my mouth where I had caught it in my fall. I looked at the beast from where I stood replacing my usual Stan Laurel expression with the forty yard stare. He was not impressed and snorted out of his nostrils while scraping one of his feet on the ground several times in quick succession like a bull before the charge, either that or the drugs had just kicked in.

Like a Hindi movie I tasted the blood with my finger and then screamed warrior like running at the creature with my arms and legs flailing about like a madman wind-milling for every last vestige of strength that I could muster in this life or death situation.

Dalj and Spiros had already leapt up after seeing me get tossed like a rag doll moments before and they watched on helplessly as I raced into the Lions den still wind-milling thin air. The beast moved his head a few times as each of my wild wind-mill strikes missed his features by inches. He was not so lucky when my back swing suddenly caught him flush in the crown jewels. I actually felt the back of my hand careering sweetly into his tackle doubling him over instantly. The rest was now easy as I stepped back a few paces and booted him as hard as I could, once again in the same spot. The sickly wounded and groaning noise that he let out even brought water to my eyes, even his friends all winced in pain for their colleague. I kicked him so hard that I am sure I saw him swirling his detached ghoulies around inside his mouth before swallowing them again before crashing to the floor unconscious. It was over and the giant had been felled for today, I was the new action hero, the new Sheriff in town.

I dusted my hands and motioned for the others to walk out behind me. I inched to the door while the other trouble makers tended to their fallen comrade. Once outside we all ran like mad and quickly found ourselves in a taxi heading back to the hotel. What a day and what a time to let out my pent up frustrations I thought. Prity hugged me tightly in the back and whispered, 'You are my hero and for that I am going to make mad, sensual love to you tonight babes.' She looked at me with the most seductive, come to bed eyes I had ever seen and I had the urge to have her right there and then. Instead, I sat back and thanked my lucky stars that everyone was safe and that there was only one more day of anguish to endure.

Chapter 16

'Roofies' delight

We entered the hotel lobby area and Dalj said that he was taking Pinto upstairs to let her lie down. She had been complaining of a headache and it seemed that the excitement of the trip was now beginning to take its toll on her. I kissed her on the cheek and she made her way up to the lift that had now been fixed, letting out a well deserved ripple of air from her butt cheeks as she shambled across the floor. They both left the area.

Spiros had hardly said a word since the service station fracas and retired to his room without further ado. This left Prity and I on the dance floor. I mentioned that I was going to get a stiff drink after the dust up I had been involved in just so that I could calm my frayed nerves. She pinched my bum cheekily and told me to be upstairs for some duvet action as soon as possible. She headed off to get herself ready for me whilst I perched myself up at the rather darkly lit bar and ordered a large brandy.

The barman slid the drink over to me and I gulped it down in one foul swoop. I ordered another and one more for the road. I lifted the final glass to my lips when in what was a moment of clarity I heard the toe cringing voice that had haunted me for eons, a sinister tone that always spelt imminent blood or danger, or a fusion of the two.

'Finally made it did you?'

I turned my head slowly and cautiously along the bar and there were a row of empty bar stools. As my eyes strained upwards I saw the angel of death standing there sipping from a tumbler perched like a sentry at the end of the bar. My guts twisted and churned, the brandy swishing around inside not assisting in this delicate dilemma. The buoyant sensation that the brandy shots had given me only moments before was now replaced with a feeling of dark fear as the face of pure evil glared back at me through the pit deep shadows of the bar. My thoughts of fornicating like a wild beast upstairs similarly expunged from my mind quicker as I stood firm, or at least tried to.

The figure stood up and slowly walked over to me, tumbler in his hand and a look of unpredictability caked over his face. It was none other than Terry, the dirty mongrel had got to me at last. I was so close to the finish line and now I was tugged back by my life long tormentor. I was in a whole pyre of faeces and really did not know which way to turn. The question was did I have the minerals to survive the next five or ten minutes? I took a deep breath and steadied myself as best I could. Terry smirked at my attempts to disguise my bursting uneasiness and agitation. I had to meet him when I was drunk, so vulnerable and disarmed, I was petrified.

'Same again?' he offered pointing to the glass in my hand. I quickly knocked back the contents of the glass and slammed the glass on the bar attempting to conceal my trepidation.

Terry laughed, 'Don't worry I am not here to harm you or anything, but I tell you it was hard to track you down.'

He handed me his tumbler and told me to drink it. I looked in the glass and saw that it contained Bacardi rum and coke. This was my usual tipple. I then saw Terry ordering another drink for himself. The barman duly obliged.

'Come on then drink up. Here is to you and your success in Bollywood.' Terry raised his glass and began to knock it back. I hesitated and could see him peering down at me through the glass. He lowered it and said, 'Come on mate let's start again shall we. I did not realise just how much you wanted to pursue your dream that's all, okay. Trust me – right?'

He seemed to have changed, it was possible and I could not detect any hostilities from him whatsoever. He turned and paid the barman for his drink and I quickly drank up, the entire lot down in a record five seconds. I was prepared to give him the benefit of the doubt, maybe he had changed for the better. Perhaps it had taken me leaving for him to realise that I suffered enough.

We then remained at the bar and chatted, albeit uneasily on my part, and I insisted on getting the next and last round of drinks in before I would retire for the evening.

Terry seemed quite relaxed about things and I asked him how he had tracked me down. Through his connections he said. It sounded shady and in reality it probably was but I did not delve any further.

Approximately twenty minutes into our chat I started to feel a tad queasy but put it down to the myriad of brandy's I had consumed in such a short space of time. The feeling began to intensify and I found myself clutching my throat. My eyes felt heavy and I could hear snatches of conversation as Terry made small talk with the barman. I knew it was time to go to my room and mumbled this to Terry as I stood up. The effects of the drinks now taking there toll on me. He assisted me and wished me a good night and that he would see me in the morning to support me for the final audition. My judgement had been sound about him. After all who ever said that a leopard could not change its spo...sp...a leop...spo...all of a sudden the room became blurry, and I rubbed my eyes. I rubbed harder and they still remained foggy and fragmented. What was happening to me? I felt nauseous and looked at the tumbler laying there incriminatingly on the bar. The one that Terry had handed to me twenty minutes ago with just enough time for the noxious substance to work its way through my system. I knew that from previous biology lessons as the same applied to food and tablets. I concluded painfully that I had been poisoned, and was going to die right here at the bar, so near to fulfilling my goal. If I could muster a wild scream I would have blown the roof up such was the turmoil I found myself in. It felt like my feet were in quicksand and that those around me were just letting me sink, rather than throwing me a stick or lifeline. I was in a desperate manner and surrounded by an evil force, one that I had stupidly under estimated much to my burgeoning peril.

I looked at Terry and his smiling manner and presence had now become menacing and outwardly poisonous. The snake had duped me, I felt myself falling off the stool. I could faintly see the barman raise his eyebrows questioning what had happened. Through misty vision, I heard Terry mumble something about too many drinks and then suddenly felt my body being dragged like a car crash dummy up towards the lobby lift. The barman was on one side and Terry was propping me up on the other side. I tried to speak and warn the barman that he was being an unwitting accessory to murder but the words stuck like glue in my mouth. The drug that the bastard had dropped into the drink was a rozzie – rohynpol and I knew I would soon be out for the count. I could not even cry such was the paralysis gripping my body at that moment. I fell into the lift and then faintly saw the doors closing. Terry looked down at me sneering and landing ferocious kicks to my mid section. I did not feel the kicks as my body had shut down to any physical sensation. Rohynopol is a legitimate drug that is used for sleep disorders as it acts fast. It is part of the valium family but has ten times more potency than its average 'roofie' cousins.

The next thing I remember is being woken up on the roof of the hotel slumped against a concrete wall at one end of the roof as splashes of water soaked my face and torso. The water was constant and I realised through my blurry eyes that Terry was standing near me with a hose squirting the water directly at me without any let up.

I tried to lift my arm to cover and protect my face but it seemed stuck to my side, the effect of the substance still keeping me conscripted to the danger I was in at the hands of a merciless warrior.

I heard uproarious laughter coming from the other side of where I was laying and it took tremendous effort to move my head to the side to glance at the hyena making the noise. I remained flabbergasted and even more dejected than I could possibly have been. It was Myleene, she had also come to join the circus act that my life had become.

'What did you give me? I squawked trying in vain to keep my eyes from drooping shut again.

'Ever heard of rohynopol? It is the right kind of poison for vermin like you,' retorted a somewhat proud Terry.

My hunch had been right and he had pretended to drink from his glass at the bar when I saw him, therefore adding to the subterfuge before handing it to me to take the full effects of the drugs.

'Don't worry you won't die, but the effects will make you sleep for a good few hours. Definitely enough time for what we need to do.' Myleene joined him and I saw their blurry frames standing in-front and looking down on me. They had worked me like a violin and now went in for the coup de grace. Myleene sunk to her knees and waved some paperwork in-front of my face.

'Now sign that and save yourself.' She lowered the paperwork to where my right hand was resting motionless on the floor and then inserted a pen in my hand.

SLAP! She whacked me across the face and I fell asleep once again.

'Sign it and we will leave you alone,' she shouted.

I managed to take a grip of the pen and even dragged it over to the bottom of the paper that she was holding. I just wanted to sign whatever it was they were waving about under my nose so that I could go to sleep once and for all.

'What am I sig…' That was the last thing I remembered before I finally drifted off for a long sleep. It was rather like having a general anaesthetic in the hospital where the nurse asks you to count back from ten. Then, like the stubborn little bastard you are, you think you are going to make it and so rattle down the numbers before slumping back like a dying goose on the pillow at a measly six, letting out a trickle of drool for that special Kodak moment as you do so.

That was all I could remember at that moment, then pitch black serenity soaked my body like a warm sponge. My last moment of being compus mentis made one thing unequivocally perspicuous to me and that was I was not sure if I would ever open my eyes to see another living day on this Earth. That was the brutal reality before I switched off for a long and nerve racking sleep. It could all be over already...

Chapter 17

Perilous sign

Saturday 18th July - SPLASH! I felt the ice cold water waking me up in a flash. I shook my head violently like any good old fashioned mutt would do after getting water on to their fur. The morning sun beamed down on my withered body and I could feel the burning rays piercing through my trousers and singing my legs. The first thing I checked for was to see if I could lift my hand up. With that minor task completed, I slowly moved my legs about and regained the motion in the little fellas'. Next, I clicked my neck and rubbed the back with my hand. It was sore from the strange position I had been left in over night.

It was then the danger of the situation the previous evening lurched up and grabbed me by the throat. I tried to stand up but slipped, but persevered and managed to regain my footing and steadied myself on the roof top ledge of the hotel. It took me a few more moments to compose my thoughts and suck in some much needed air. At this altitude the air was fresh and clean. I filled my nostrils with as much as I could before blowing out of my mouth. I sensed the oxygen meandering its way to my frazzled brain cells and activating them like electrical charges.

I then turned to search for the stairway so that I could return to my room. I stopped in my tracks, there standing like end of level guardians in any good computer game were Terry and Myleene. They had seen everything and had just been waiting before pouncing on me like the vultures they were.

There was no escape, I looked over my shoulder, and was met with a sheer drop of at least two hundred feet. I did not feel that my Bat fink super powers would be up to the task of fending them off and then flying off the roof top in heroic glory. I remained frozen to the spot and far too emasculated to put up any form of feeble resistance.

Terry stepped forward holding some papers in his hand and spoke, 'We had to wait all night for you to get your act together. Now do you want to sign these papers?' Myleene was standing behind him and hanging around like a bad smell.

'What do you want me to sign? I asked knowing exactly what it was they were after.

'Give us the money or you will be going over the ledge it is as simple as that.'

Terry's threat was the human equivalent of lock jaw and his teeth were truly sunk into my arm and he was not about to let go.

'Yeah you useless piece of shit, do something good in your life for once and think about all the sacrifices that we had to endure bringing you up.' Myleene summed up her obvious disdain towards me with her jaundiced attack.

Terry slammed the paperwork in my chest and handed me a pen with his other hand. I took hold of the papers and the pen before scrutinising the contents as fast as I could given the threat hanging over me like the Sword of Damocles. It was a straight forward legal document authorising full payment of the funds to my carers. It stated that I granted them power of attorney over the money contained within my account. I reluctantly signed the document and the accompanying bank details allowing for a simple bacs transaction. My whole world was crumbling like a house of cards. I always knew that human behaviour was fragile and subject to startling change subject to the situation, but to this day I had not accounted for just how ruthless people could be when it came to money. They were willing to toss me over the ledge for my money and the very thought was inconceivable.

What did they see in one another apart from being thieving toe rags? Terry was a born thug and with his recent drinking splurges had brought out the inner demon in him.

The dirty deed was accomplished and they examined the papers assessing whether I had attempted to hoodwink them by signing off as Donald Duck or something as extravagant. They were not disappointed and with that Terry moved up close and personal causing me to shuffle back a few paces until I met resistance in the shape of the ledge.

'Now if you consider trying to stop this payment, or opening your big gob about what has happened, then I promise you I will kill you. No sorrow and no delay – you will be dead, understand?'

The guy was inhumane and to coin a phrase that I had heard Dalj use on several occasions when the proverbial had hit the fan – '*my bond was parti*' (my arsehole was ripped).

'Just tell me how you found me. Who told you where I was?' I needed to know for old times sake.

'Well lets just put it this way I can be very convincing and that weasel Visperal, you know your drama teacher ended up in a coma for withholding details from me.'

I was shocked, how could he have done this to him? He was harmless.

'Oh yeah, all he had to do was tell me, but he wanted me to torture him first, so hey I am never one to let an opportunity pass.' Terry threw another malicious log on to the fire as he flexed his skills as a raconteur.

'A coma?' I clarified, appalled by what I had heard.

'Sleeping like a baby.' he snarled back at me.

Terry grilled me for a few more sinister moments about which bank to go to in India and who I had spoken with already at the bank. I did not hold back and gave both of them as much information as they needed to get them out of my life forever. I heard him mention to Myleene that they would clear the bank out and then book the next flight back to London.

They then left but before exiting the roof, Terry turned to me and muttered, 'In case you are wondering, this money is owed to us so I don't feel at all bad about it. Secondly you fucking loser, get yourself a new pad when you get back to Britain, cos you ain't living with us again.'

They were gone much to my relief. This journey had taught me that there were a lot of unscrupulous people in this world and Wayne and Waynetta (Terry and Myleene) were no exceptions to the rule.

I waited about five minutes to ensure that they had disappeared and then rapidly headed downstairs to my hotel room. I used my key and opened the door. Inside my gorgeous girl was fast asleep in the bed. It appeared that she had waited for me last night and then fallen asleep from over tiredness.

I looked at the time, it was only five a.m, which meant by my calculations that I had been knocked out for a matter of hours. I rummaged around in the room, casually glancing up to the ceiling and smirked to myself. After all, I felt lucky to still be alive. Downstairs I heard the faint sounds of police sirens blaring and then cutting out. There seemed to be some kind of commotion in the street and I could see officers mingling outside through the window of my room.

At that moment Prity started to wake up. She saw me by the window, 'Hey babe why are you up so early? She asked curiously. The poor thing had not realised that I had just spent the good part of the night freezing my knackers off on the roof top of the darned hotel.

I did not have the energy to give her a warts and all break down of the kind of nightmare I had endured and so moved away from the window and sat beside her hugging her, whilst trying to stay away from being overcome by her grotesque morning breath.

She knew something was wrong, 'Why are you wet? What's happened? Where have you been?' She sprayed the questions at me with a verbal Uzi. The Spanish inquisition continued for another five minutes before I stopped her and decided that I would have to explain myself to avoid another fusillade of probes.

BANG! BANG! I jumped out of my skin as several shots sounded from down in the street. There was a pervading atmosphere of trouble and doom in the air and I sensed that I would be tasting the local hospital food very soon. I looked at Prity and a flicker of fear ran across her face, her hands began to shake and I knew we were in deep and troubled waters.

Chapter 18

Hidden treasure

'What the hell was that?' screamed Prity as she clung on to me for dear life. The noise of what appeared to be a gun sounding was startling. I quickly looked out of the window and saw more police officers congregating below. It appeared that a local criminal had been locking horns with the local sheriffs and on further supposition, I realised that the criminal had been eviscerated in his tracks by a trigger happy marksman. This was what I fed back to Prity and she felt more relaxed. I continued where I had left off with my explanation.

Then for the next half an hour, I told her all about the ambush and how I had tried my best to survive. I naturally added some needed 'masala' into the story and she seemed devastated by what she had heard.

'Why did you feel you couldn't tell me? she asked seemingly annoyed at my reservations about upsetting her.

'I didn't want to upset you anymore than needed especially after what we have both been through together on this wild and crazy journey.'

She nodded acknowledging the reasoning behind my reticence in reciting my ordeal when I had returned from the jaws of death up there on the precarious roof.

'But you have just given them the money. Are you not upset by this? It was money that was owed to you from your parents. Surely, you are not giving it up that easy and without a fight. Are you?'

She was right. What kind of imbecile would have just let that kind of money slip though his fingers? It was insane and I tried to explain to her that I had no choice but to sign the document after I had been drugged. She did not understand and began lambasting me for being so nonchalant about it all.

'You are kidding me right? she said disappointingly.

'Yeah, well kind of.' I replied.

'What do you mean, kind of?'

'Well, I did sign the document there is no denying that. I signed it and handed it back to them to go and loot my riches from the bank. But, I forgot to mention was that I had already taken the money out of the bank before. Smart hey?' I was sitting in the Jacuzzi of smugness and puffing a cigar of sly.

'That is cute. When did you get the money out? Prity asked suitably impressed with my outfoxing antics.

'That day when we returned from visiting the Swami, I nipped into the bank with Dalj in the car and took all the money out and hid it.'

Prity's mouth opened in sheer delight. She shook her head and said cautiously, 'Well done for staying one step ahead but be careful because there are equally smart people around like that animal Anil and Baldip. Just be careful, okay,' her words carried cautionary weight.

'I will honey don't worry. I am not as naïve enough as to put it under the bed or anything, trust me okay. We just need to get through this last day together and then I will make sure that no-one finds us ever again.'

'I know, I pray to God we can make it home together, and I swear I will kiss the tarmac at Heathrow if we get that far. But, please just tell me one thing are you sure you are okay after what happened?'

'Yeah babes I am fine.' I felt almost exultant in victory after giving Terry and Myleene the slip.

'Just focus on the dream, you and me, a nice cottage somewhere and a bag full of money. What more could we ask for after this journey. And, you never know if things go my way today you may even be hooked up with a superstar.' We both laughed.

There was a knock on the door and it was Dalj standing there in his finest jimmy jams.

'Did you hear that noise? I think it was shots being fired.' he surmised.

'I know it was a whole load of officers downstairs sorting out some kind of situation, but it is done now.'

'Right let me get dressed and I will go see,' he said turning on a six pence ready get changed.

'NO! I shouted back at him stopping him dead in his tracks.

'I mean, don't go, it could be dangerous and you know what some of these foreign countries are like. If you turn up to have a look they would sooner fit you up so that they can close the crime scene down then let the puzzle of letting it go unsolved.'

Dalj agreed and mentioned that we would probably have to start getting ready in any case as the decision for the weeks auditions was taking place in a matter of hours. He went back to his room and Prity and I started to dress in our finest ensemble. Despite knowing that the writing was on the wall with regards to the decision I still wanted to present myself in the best possible light and go out with the necessary bang. Pride and fortitude were my two by words this day and both I prayed would assist me machete my way through the jungle of chaos the week had been for us all.

After getting dressed, we met the others downstairs for breakfast. I had booked our rooms for an additional set of hours at the hotel as we had an evening flight, and so reserved our packing for tonight.

This time at the table downstairs there was no sign of Baldip, as I had earlier discharged him from his duties with us. Spiros was running a little late and se we waited patiently for him in the outside area of the restaurant catching our breakfast al fresco in our time honoured fashion.

Whilst we waited, I could see Dalj asking questions of the hotel staff regarding the gun shots that we had heard before. One waiter, Gupta Patel, explained how the police had received a tip off about some criminals operating at the hotel and when they confronted the group, they turned on them and tried to take hostages and fight back using knives and other such implements.

He went on to say that the group were subdued and once in custody reinvigorated their attack which led to the fatal shots that killed them. I almost punched the air in exhilaration when I heard the news. I was utterly convinced that Anil had been killed in the fire fight as he was the only one skulking around with his cronies in the hotel and criminally would have stuck out like a sore thumb. I whispered this to Dalj and he appeared equally content. Ding dong the wicked witch was dead, now all I needed to do was get the feedback from the audition, avoid the comeback from Terry and Myleene, and leave the country. I was also desperate to find out what condition Visperal Canchita was in back home. The guy was like a father figure for me and without him this Bollywood break would never have happened. Gupta then walked off leaving us all to speculate who the slain victims were. He had said there was a criminal group and this fed into all manner of hypothesis and guess work.

Spiros joined us, as did Pinto. I felt that I had a spring in my step for the first time. The thought of Terry and Myleene going to withdraw the money at the bank and ending up with nothing was good, but the thought of Anil meeting his maker in a fire fight with the police was lip smacking to say the least.

It was too good to be true and kick started my day like a triple espresso.

This time we hailed down a taxi to take us for the final time in this particular week to the famous studios.

Whilst we waited, Dalj pointed over to a series of vehicles parked in the far reaches of the hotel complex, 'Hey isn't that Baldip's minibus over there?' I looked over and saw the rear end of a minibus poking out and sitting snugly between other vehicles, and must admit it looked similar. No sooner had we began speaking about this when our taxi arrived.

We crammed into it like sardines with Spiros sitting at the front and the four of us, Pinto, Dalj, Prity and I squeezed in the rear with a monumental effort. Every bump and pot hole in the road making me shoot up head first slamming into the roof of the vehicle like an Exorcet missile. I was not amused.

The closer we got to the studios, the more it dawned on me that the day had finally arrived when I would discover my acting fate. I was riddled with nerves and my sphincter was twitching faster than a rabbit's nose. It all boiled down to this. The next chapter of my career was going to be ceremoniously concluded in a matter of hours. My biggest threat was to avoid the nefarious clutches of Terry and Myleene after they would meet with disappointment at the local bank. My tactics were to remain in public places until that time and to stealthily retrieve our bags after the studio visit and safely get on the plane for the return journey home. It seemed clear enough but I knew that there were a plethora of land mines that I would need to negotiate between now and that metaphorical finishing line. Like the Swami had predicted to me earlier; *'Be very careful, someone is going to get you and the fire will not tell me the outcome, but I see blood and danger, lots of blood and real terrible danger for you. Watch your back or it will be over.'*

I held on to these thoughts as my haggard eyes honed in on Spiros sitting in front of me.

The words blood and danger echoed in my ears, then an epiphany, my eyes widened in disbelief, maybe it was Spiros who was the one to watch. My heart thumped wildly and my gulp was audible for all to hear. I was even more afraid as the taxi trundled closer to our destination...

Chapter 19

Judgement day

Once again, we entered the mouth watering utopia of Film City. The complex was as devilishly sexy and inviting as it had always been. I yearned for this opportunity more than I could express in words. I saw the other aspiring actors assembling in the main acting arena. I left the others behind at the back and walked the green mile to my seat. The butterflies were swarming around in my stomach. It was D-day and a sense of impending failure was always close to me. A stagehand appeared at the front and began to call the register with his Indian twang amusing some of the less educated amongst us. Then there was one guy who kept asking questions at every given opportunity, he was some freak show from the darkest depths of Luton and there he was, arm up question, arm up question. There is always one wet back who has to act like the smart Alec, and here he was living up to his smarmy reputation.

Spiros sat a few seats away from me and was in contemplative thought. His face a sweaty and doom laden mess. We exchanged a nervous glance every now and then as the waiting continued. He looked as though his soufflé had already collapsed. He fidgeted, took deep breaths and kept rubbing his hands and wiping away the sweat from his forehead. Actually seeing his squirming disposition lifted my soul under the veils of speckled doom. I had started the day running on red, stuttering splattering my way through the events that unfolded the previous evening, but now I was being refuelled by virtue of witnessing the great warrior Spiros allowing the ubiquitous adrenaline monster poke a steely fist up his jacksy and jiggle it about for fun. He exuded the optimism and virility of a dead corpse and I was loving every god damn second of the spectacle.

CLAP! CLAP!

My entertainment was cut short when an immaculately dressed, eloquent and well heeled elderly gentleman appeared on the stage to address the audience. Who was this guy? I was about to find out.

'Welcome, you are probably all wondering how you have performed in the weeks auditions and whether or not one has landed a role in the film '*The Valati.*'

I listened intently, it was the moment of truth and this was the king of banana skins a gun shot away.

'Now before I proceed with the results and confirmed call backs. I need to highlight a serious issue to you and one that it is best felt shared with young recipients like your good selves who are attempting to break into this prestigious industry.'

We all looked at one another baffled. I turned and looked at Prity and she shrugged her shoulders in resignation. No-one in the arena had any idea what was going on.

Suddenly the wall of confusion was broken, the quantum of cogitating solitude shattered.

'Jaspal has been arrested for various offences and will never set foot in this industry again.'

It was a water cooler moment. My Brokeback mountain amigo had been swifted and was not even allowed back into the studios after years of dedicated practice and commitment. His crime was soon evident to the non believers and critics sat around me.

'He was supplying drugs, soliciting prostitution, and quite frankly he was corrupt.'

The words sledge hammered home to all of us and immediately prompted feverish chatter amongst the crowd that had gathered from every part of the set.

The groomed gentleman added, 'Now that means the movie will be getting a new director.' He paused and scanned our faces, 'That director will be me – Sunil Kapoor.'

He let this sink in and paced on the stage for a few moments. He returned to the same spot and went on, Fortunately, you will not have to perform again as I have managed to see video footage of the auditions that you had. This is a routine thing that we have here at the studios and it has assisted us in the past to sort out the difficult cases, especially when one or two actors have gone down to the wire.'

There was a cheer of relief from all of us. It meant that we were spared the agonising prospect of having to act out the same debilitating scenes for a new director.

'Okay here are the results for parts in the film.' He proceeded to open an envelope. I looked back once more and Prity and Dalj were both crossing their fingers for me and I could see Pinto on the floor reciting some kind of holy prayer, rocking back and forth whilst mumbling something under her breath. They say you are only as strong as your entourage in these kind of scenarios, and I felt that I was blessed.

'In third place and playing a supporting role in The Valati is…' He read the card he was holding, 'JIMMY. A huge cheer went up again and Jimmy, a budding competitor of mine leapt up and joined the new director on stage, shaking his hand and then being ushered to the side of him. He looked at the card again, 'In second place and playing the main supporting role to The Valati is….' I closed my eyes and prayed. The pause lingered for what seemed like an eternity.

'Is TONY.' The scrawny arsehole had nicked a spot on the film. The bloke was a non entity and a complete waste of skin and sinew.

Spiros held his head in his hands and I sat back knowing that my chance had withered away like a puff of smoke.

'The final place and playing the lead role as The Valati goes to…' I gulped hard as though I was swallowing a bee.

'I guess I don't have to read the card for this one, it is easy. He has been outstanding all week. The Valati is…SAM MIERS.' I jumped up from my seat with both hands in the air. I was stunned, it was a moment of pure magic. The remaining guys clapped profusely and I was hugged and congratulated by everyone. I looked back and my entourage were equally ecstatic. Prity gave me a thumbs up while she fielded a call on her mobile, she looked quite rattled but there would be more time to discover who was annoying her later, for this was my moment in the sun and I was ready to bask in it for as long as I could.

Spiros began to walk off in disgust, kicking a few chairs as he left. His titanic efforts at brown nosing had nose dived on him. He was not happy stomping off somewhere to lick his wounds.

'WAIT!' screamed Sunil Kapoor. Spiros stopped where he was and looked up hopefully.

'Also, a bonus place goes to…SPIROS!

His eyes lit up like stars, he was in the film and his patent delight was there for all to witness.

'Who will be playing the part of Santoshy – the kusra (transvestite) in two scenes in the film.'

We all collapsed in fits of hysterics. Pinto at the back had been told what had happened and started to jive and jig on her own, clapping and hissing at the comedy. The laughter roared on with Spiros, humiliated left standing on his own without any lasting credibility. He stormed off in an angry huff, smashing through the side doors to the arena.

I was led on to the stage and the congratulations and adulation was mind blowing. The pats on the back, compliments, and plaudits were coming at me thick and fast. Whilst the manic celebrations on the stage were in full throttle, I caught a glimpse of Dalj and raised a triumphant fist to him, a gesture that he reciprocated. Prity had only just lowered the mobile phone from her ear and delightedly waved at me from the back of the arena. Some music then sounded and the stage hands began to dance. Sunil whispered, 'Don't worry it is traditional when someone lands a big part in a movie. Go, enjoy yourself.'

I thanked him for giving me the opportunity.

'What happens now?' I asked.

'You will return to the UK and will be sent a contract which you will sign. Filming then commences in two months time. Be ready because you will be in India for one moths filming on set locations.'

He then stepped back clapping his hands.

'YESSSSSSS!' I screamed and immediately began performing the funky chicken dance with some stage guy, who after the first few seconds of fun, stood away and looked at me with freakish admiration as I flapped my imaginary wings in my cocoon of happiness. I swivelled like John Travolta and whistled to Dalj. I could see that he was busy enjoying himself doing Bhangra with an equally joyful Pinto.

They were doing the rail guddi together and other wonderful Bhangra routines as Pinto unleashed the inner diva in her. It seemed that they were both lost in the magic of the moment too. I looked on fully satiated when suddenly my jaw hit the stage when Dalj, without warning scooped Pinto up, leaving her legs dangling over his arms while he supported her body in the cradled position. He then began to swing her around his body, round she whirled shouting 'chuttay maatay, chuttay maatay,' she screamed like a child whilst trying desperately to keep her dentures firmly within her mouth. Suddenly, her satisfied look was replaced with one of outright and crashing horror.

Dalj the silly fox had got carried away swinging dear old Pinto like the madman he was and had not seen the raised shelving sticking out next to where they were sat. The last thing I lucidly remember is seeing Pinto's terrified and bamboozled *'why me'* face as Dalj slammed her head straight into the shelving with a wildly sickening crunching sound echoing around the arena. I recoiled in horror as did the others who had witnessed the near decapitation. I raced over as Pinto writhed around on the floor in knee jolting agony uttering words to the effect of, 'Pinto margee, Pinto margee,' (meaning she is dead). Her Bollywood vacation was all but over save for the epitaph being engraved in her blood. The buzzard certainly had one foot in the casket and was either set to go home in a body bag or via the local hospital. I rebuked Dalj for being so immature and he kept saying sorry umpteen times whilst crouching down tending to the battered fallen hero.

After receiving some medical attention from the ambulance crew who had arrived several minutes later, they diagnosed her as fit and well despite some lacerations to the side of her head where she had caught the shelving.

Meanwhile Prity kept congratulating and kissing me and saying that she could not believe that I had actually done it, she was just about as surprised as me I tell you.

I then asked Prity if she was okay about the call that she had fielded when I was up on the stage.

She said that she took the opportunity to call the drama school back in the UK to find out the progress of Visperal, and if he had regained consciousness from his coma. She went on to say that staff at the drama school indicated that he was improving and that it was an unprovoked attack by an unknown assailant. She said that this news had distressed her and that she felt helpless being here. Prity always stayed behind to have a coffee with us after my acting classes, and as such got to know Visperal very well, so I understood her plight. I hugged her and told her it would be okay as we would be back home in the UK this time tomorrow. She smiled back at me.

'Right that's it then, mission accomplished let's go home and celebrate the contract.' I said to the others.

We walked and talked as we made our way steadily to the taxi rank outside.

'Wait what about Spiros? Dalj enquired.

'What about him? He can stew for all I care,' said Prity.

'He will come when he is good and ready. I say now we get back to the hotel, get our bags, taxi it to the airport and get the flipping hell out of Dodge.' I could not have been any more direct with my plan of action.

'We need to stay on our guard in case Terry and Myleene are waiting at the hotel. Why don't you go in first and see if the coast is clear,' I said to Dalj.

'No sweat, done!' he replied like a seasoned war veteran.

Then as we sat in the taxi ready to return to the hotel, I saw a shadowy flash in the corner of my eye. My spatial awareness training had come in handy and I knew there was trouble on the horizon. I looked but it was too late, Spiros was by the side of the taxi, fists clenched and looking agitated. He moved his chin from side to side as you do when you are preparing to throw hands with someone, it looked as though the poo fairy had just crapped in his mouth as he grunted and growled outside. He waited by the side of the car staring at Pinto pressing her nose against the window and pulling faces. I knew I had to face him one time and so like *'Johnny bad arse'* I got out of the car, walked around and stood toe to toe with the bruiser. I had to see if he was made of as stern stuff as he had led me to believe. There comes a time in every guy's life when you can scream and shout as much as you like, but you have to back up what you are saying. So here I was a maggot on a stick for him, all he had to do was blow on my face and I am certain he would have knocked me over like a ten pin. My bravado was a smokescreen to test his mettle. I was a duck above the surface but in reality, my legs were flapping wildly out of sight under the water.

He raised his fist and I braced myself for the blow that was going to give me an instant set of piano teeth. He moved his hand to my quivering body and opened it suddenly, this jolted me backwards a few steps. I looked down at his hand and it was extended in the form of a handshake.

'I guess I can hate on you for the rest of your days, but what is the point. I guess the best man won on the day. There will always be other auditions and so I will see you around. Oh and good luck with it all.'

I grabbed his hand and we shook like adults.

'So what now, I mean for you?' I asked.

'I am extending my stay here in this beautiful country. I am going to be like David Carradine, just take some time out and walk the plains of this paradise.'

His ideology of relaxation seemed perfect. We parted at this point with the group all letting bygones be bygones and wishing him well. We watched as he trotted off along the dusty road following the signs to the beach, kicking some stray pebbles along the way. The great Spiros had been magnanimous in defeat and just like that he disappeared out of view never to be seen again.

I turned to get back in the car and could see a rumpus in the back with Pinto wielding her chappal and striking the taxi driver about the head several times with Dalj and Prity trying in vain to control her arms and deflecting some of the blows. The taxi driver looked annoyed ducking his head out of the spitfire of blows raining down on him like a fiery shower. Dalj quickly explained that Pinto had mistakenly accused the driver as being the one responsible for smashing her head before. Everyone then settled down and we set off. Dalj remained quiet for the rest of the journey fearing that Pinto would realise that he was actually the head smashing executioner saddled up next to her. Prity remained pensive, she was thinking about Visperal and no doubt the rollercoaster that this trip had sent us all on. Our emotions had been churned up and spat out at every turn. I closed my eyes for a siesta with the thought that I had fulfilled everything I had set out to achieve, with one more hurdle to negotiate back at the hotel. This was going to be the toughest test of them all and we all knew it...

Chapter 20

Knock knock

We arrived at the hotel, mentally drained, battered and bruised from the entire week. I rolled out of the taxi like an OAP. The others followed behind. I felt a wave of exuberance walking into the hotel foyer, it was though the persistent foot on my throat had been lifted and my spirit had finally been let loose. I notified the hotel staff standing behind the reception desk that we would be checking out within a few minutes so that they could prepare any invoices for us. We marched to the lift and up we went, the taste of success coursing through my veins and even swirling around in the saliva in my mouth.

Dalj and Pinto ducked into their room while we went to ours. Dalj had mentioned that they had more or less already packed and that he would come to our room once he had finished.

Just before entering my room I turned around to Prity and took her in my arms snogging her full on the lips with a pouting smacker that Don Juan would have been proud of in his day. She kissed me back and our tonsil hockey session lasted for a matter of seconds with the crotch of my trousers rising to the occasion.

'Come on, we had better get ready to go,' she said gently pushing me off and turning me around to open the door.

Upon entering my eyes almost popped out of my head, my room had been turned upside down, ransacked like you would not believe. I looked anxiously across our belongings as they were strewn around the floor. There were underpants hanging off of the light shade, Prity's make up thrown about everywhere and all of our belongings raped and defiled. I could smell cannabis in the air where the burglars had been smoking away leisurely whilst stripping us of our dignity. It had all the hallmarks of that bastard Terry I scowled to Prity.

She screamed in shock and subsequently broke down in tears. I stepped further in the room to survey the damage the burglars had caused. My hopes of a bourgeois life were dramatically dashed looking around at the butchery of our prized accoutrements before me.

We stood there devastated and it had all the hall marks of something that Terry would have done after being humiliated at the bank. I felt the waters rising in my inner chamber of dread and an air of awful conception rapidly filling inside me. Why did Terry feel it necessary to punish me in this way? What was his motivation? Was this his way of teaching me a lesson? These and similar unanswered questions shuttled back and forth across the loom of my mind.

Whichever way I scrutinised what had happened I could sense that a palpable fear stalked the room with its tactile claws prodding and taunting our hapless souls. I flicked my eyes up at the ceiling and breathed a sigh of relief. The ceiling squares were all intact and I was thankful for this small crumb of comfort for it was the very place that I had carefully ensconced the money that day after I had returned from visiting the Swami. I had stood on a chair and meticulously placed the bag in one of the square partitions in the ceiling so that it would be safe from this kind of ransacking violation. My calculations had been correct and I knew that they had not found the money because the chair in the room was in exactly the same position I had left it earlier that morning.

But, where were they now?

Dalj pushed the door open behind us and entered the room with Pinto straddling behind him, still looking a trifle unsteady on her feet after her concussing blow to her cranium.

'What has happened here mate?' he looked as demoralised as Prity and I.

Prity sat on the bed and sifted through what was left of her cosmetics on the bed, weeping and letting out mouse like whimpers as she picked up each individual item for closer inspection.

My shock was rapidly beginning to be replaced with insatiable fury. When without warning a sinister and unwelcome voice peppered the air, 'Ahh, here they are the Brady Bunch, all together under one roof.'

The voice hit me straight between the eyes.

'Yeah, the star is here. You really should be up on the stage, fucking sweeping it up that is, ha ha.'

Suddenly, the toilet door flung open and out from his lair stepped the ball breaking and reproachful foe, a hostile force that had haunted me for the duration of the trip courting a face like a dented skip. It was Anil stampeding his way resolutely back into our lives, but this time he was armed with a revolver.

'But, I thought you were dead? I said perplexed.

'The shots I heard downstairs, the criminal gang that the waiter told us about. It had to be you.' My questions lacked the evidential value that I had hoped for.

Anil scratched the side of his head with the tip of the gun.

'Sam boy. It will take something special to get rid of me. I am the kind of guy who gives Keyser Soze nightmares,' he fired back at me.

A more pungent whiff followed him out of the toilet, a smell redolent of someone having indulged in the Devil's lettuce, smoking hash whilst carrying out the Devil's work.

This parasite had shit in my coat pocket one too many times and my fists clenched and unclenched several times with my body urging me to lunge at him and to duke it out once and for all. I knew instantly that if I mistimed my attack it would have been sayonara, au revoir and shalom to my pitiful existence.

The shooting spree that I had heard was not in fact Anil but something unrelated, this was my faux pas and one that had caused me to lower my guard at the most critical of times. It was one lesson that I would not walk away from, that was evident.

'Now get in,' he waved the gun at Dalj and Pinto who both hovered by the door hoping to intercept the butcher of Mumbai with a blitzkrieg pincer movement assisted by us on the other side. This wishful thinking was dashed furthermore when a brutish looking henchman waltzed in through the open door. He stood there blocking out the light and glared directly at me. My groan could be heard for several miles when it dawned on me that the six foot five man monster was the same Hell's angel guy who had deliberately picked a fight with us at the service station when I had sacked Baldip.

It became clear to me that the pestiferous group had been following our minibus, and were sent in to pick a fight to keep us raddled with tension and fear. The tactic had clearly worked a treat, with only a mammoth effort of me squeezing my butt cheeks together preventing a trickle of diarrhoea type faeces from escaping and driving a nail in my street cred before I died at the hands of the gun wielding thug.

Right at this moment, I would have given all the tea in India to own a pair of ruby slippers just so that I could have clicked them to get out of this spiralling disaster movie that I was embroiled in.

The huge beast flashed me the kind of smile that intimated subtly that he was going to eat me with his chips after Anil had finished putting the squeeze on me, snapping me out of my weakened and persistent vegetative frame of mind. I had already switched off because I knew unquestionably that Anil was going to execute each and every one of us after he had mugged me of the money he so desperately sought.

'Anil, please, I just want to go home.' I muttered sounding like a wounded hippo.

He laughed hard and leaned against the wall, flicking his eyes at the thug and indicating for him to lock the door, which he did immediately.

'Give me the money and I will make sure you die without suffering,' he hissed.

With that statement, I knew that I was a cast away stranded on his Island of Evil.

'But, it is not here, it is in the bank.' I tried the bluff testing the water with my big toe.

'Did you see the word circus written on the door when you came in today?' he asked.

I did not understand and remained quiet.

'Did you? he snapped.

'Err no.' I replied nervously.

'Yeah, well then stop treating me like a clown and give me the fucking money or I will torture you right here and now,' he growled.

I could now smell the gun powder filling my nostrils the closer Anil inched towards me, when in the click of a finger, Pinto suddenly and unpredictably snapped into life moving forward and lunging at the thug, almost hovering in the air in a Matrix style pose with her chunni flapping underneath her. It seemed as though she remained suspended for a few seconds in mid air before she leapt on to the thug and started to grapple with the henchman biting into his arm with her dentures. That was the trouble, she did not realise the imminent danger that she was in through such life threatening actions. She clung on with her mouth firmly wrapped around the bruisers' forearm like a Pitball terrier whilst he desperately tried to wrestle her off. Her eyes were like burning mists of blood and it was like a good old saloon fight in a Western movie. Dalj also waded into the cesspit of violence by punching the thug's arms with his best shots, he may as well have gone for a Chinese burn on his wrists as the punches merely brushed off him unconvincingly.

The entire fracas was a waste as there should have been cameras rolling and catching the mayhem unfold, it would have made great TV with the soon to be real life dead bodies thrown in for added razzmatazz. The barn burner raged on like a classic Bollywood film when suddenly Dalj, like a beaver on ecstasy pills launched himself in front of me when he saw Anil raise his gun in my direction. He flew like Superman across the room so that he could take the bullet in his chest rather than let me die, whilst simultaneously shouting, 'Nayyyyyheeeeeee.' This was the make up of the man, a loyal, stellar and platinum friend. I mean there were dogs out there that could have learnt a trick or two from him in the loyalty stakes.

I recoiled in horror with the sight of Dalj hurtling towards me like a missile, arms and legs flailing and fear etched all over his face. He had got his compass back to front and instead of landing squarely in front of me he flew by crashing into the bed side lampshade smashing it to smithereens and landing with a bone breaking crunch. Anil watched this whilst still holding the gun at my head from a distance. Seconds after Dalj had humiliated himself the thug finally shrugged Pinto off by slapping her across the face knocking her out cold on the floor. I could sense that he did not want to hit an old lady but even a beast of that size felt it a necessary evil under the circumstances. Pinto lay there sprawled out on her back, minus the toe tag which was an inevitable conclusion after the trauma the wily biddy had put her body through in recent incidents. The blow had been so ferocious that I knew that she would have done well to survive it and if I had to put money on it, I guessed that the gentle old buzzard was as dead as a Dodo. My heart cried for her, she had meant no-one any harm and now she was being carried by the angels in a carriage to the astral and salubrious plains of heavenly serenity. My anger was boiling over and I was chomping at the bit to land one squarely on the jut jawed chin of the flamer huffing and puffing like *'Frankie big nuts.'*

Prity sat in a coiled up ball in the far corner of the bed during all of this and was shaking all the while. She had never been subjected to the kind of ordeal she had witnessed and sat in petrified and muted silence. I did not blame her. After all the brawling was done and dusted and everything had settled down, Anil shook his head, 'Now we all done are we?'

He was a thorn in my side and an incomparable ball buster and now he was deadly serious. In these final moments of my life, I realised painfully that we had all given it our best shot and tried to fight back despite the odds. I knew that looking at Pinto on the floor, Prity whimpering behind me and Dalj curled up by the broken lamp shade that our will and execution did not prevail and proved all but futile, but despite this it had been worth the tears and mammoth effort right up until these last poignant moments.

'Where is the money for the final time?'

He cocked the gun and held it at waist level pointing the tip at my face. This stance with the gun was a definite indication that he had killed before or received some kind of training with a firearm. When someone holds it by their waist and points it at you, it demonstrates proficiency with the gun. Firstly, it steadies their aim with the elbow nestling snugly into the body, secondly, it prevents heroic lunges for the weapon as happens in the movies, and thirdly, it improves accuracy when the gun is fired with the bullet travelling in a linear trajectory when the gun kicks back. With this quick analysis of the situation, I knew my time was up.

'It is up there,' I said reluctantly pointing to one of the partitions in the ceiling.

Anil raised his eyes up and a moon beam type smile cropped up on his gait.

'Up there, all this time it was up there. You sly kuta.' He looked rather amused by this revelation.

'Get it,' he ordered flashing the gun at me again.

I looked back at Prity for some reassurance and saw that she was still shaking. She slowly motioned with her head for me to comply with the instructions. I guessed she too realised the danger that permeated our existence at this tumultuous time.

I moved the chair to the centre of the room under the watchful eye of Anil in this butt clenching moment being careful not to make any sudden movements with my shaky hands. I stood on the chair pushing a ceiling partition up with one hand and rummaging around with my other hand before removing the Holy Grail. I stepped back down and threw the bag of money angrily at Anil. He caught it in his hand and then tossed it to the thug to inspect. The score was one nil to evil with the good team merely sucking on the orange pips at half time.

The thug opened the bag and jangled the bag of notes in his hand. He smiled and then nodded his head at Anil confirming that he held the treasure trove they so badly searched for before in his grubby little mitts.

'Now that wasn't so hard was it? he teased.

'Right get over there,' he told me to get to the back of the room where I was certain I would be executed all for just wanting to pursue my life long dream.

I shuffled over to the window and saw the thug stepping over Pinto to join me. My mind was racing and I had never been so scared in my entire life. What was going to happen? How was this going to end for me? My body shook and twitched uncontrollably. I did not want to die. What had it all been about? Pinto was out cold, I was not sure if she was dead or alive, Dalj was a dribbling mess in one corner of the room and Prity remained frozen in the same spot she had been in from the beginning of this charade. My curtain was finally coming down. I then felt the brute force of the thug restrain my arms behind my back with cable wire and then he trussed up my legs, finally placing tape over my mouth. He sat me down in a chair in the corner of the room and ordered Dalj to come and sit near me. He was tied up in the same manner as me. He then dragged Pinto by her arms and dumped her slumbering body next to us. I was uncertain as to what was going on. It all became clear in the next few moments.

Anil placed his gun down on the table where the TV was sat on and walked over to the bed.

'Now it is time for the real trophy,' he said lecherously looking at my baby girl cowering in the corner.

'I have always fancied a bit ever since I first saw you and now daddy wants his piece. The perfect end to a perfect day.' His evil knew no bounds and the thug laughed in tandem with Anil.

'She is far too cute to be with you mate, you know that. She needs a real man, like me.'

Prity's eyes widened as the realisation of what was about to occur hit her on the chin.

Anil hovered like the quintessential seasoned rapist by the foot of the bed with the raging horn, looking as though he had just downed a cocktail of horny goat weed and Viagra.

I struggled like a tethered bull to break myself free from my restraints and save my girl form what I feared the most. My muffled screaming and shouting was barely audible through the gag placed over my mouth. The more I struggled violently the more I felt my self respect and dignity go hurtling out of the window.

This was not happening to me? I writhed around in the chair. There was no stemming the flow of my tears.

They had burst through the dams completely drenching my face and turning it into a soggy mess.

The henchman kept a steely hand on my shoulder and kept me in my seat. His actions prevented me from hopping over to the bed like a kangaroo and trying to comically head butt our way out of this nightmare. The thug then took a firm grip of my hair with his other hand and turned my face to watch what was about to happen to my precious Prity. I struggled but he was far too strong.

Anil was by now on the bed and had ruthlessly dragged Prity by her heels over to him, ripping her skirt in the process and over powering her. He was as strong as an ox and her struggles were no match for him. She kept shouting for him to stop and saying 'No' over and over but he was already on top of her and the violation and rape began. I closed my eyes and prayed that this was just some kind of sick nightmare. I was wrong as I could hear her muffled sobbing and vigorous thrusting from Anil breaking my heart into a million pieces.

There was nothing that I could do to help her and felt so guilty having asked her to come on this journey - and all for what? So that she could be raped in a dingy hotel room by some diseased street urchin. It was too much to bear and I tried to block out the grunting sound that I could hear. It was sick and inhumane.

I then heard an earth shattering 'aaaaahhhhhhh,' as the final thrust from the banging porn star satisfied the perverted beast on the bed.

I slowly opened my eyes and saw Anil satisfyingly climbing off of her and zipping up his trousers in the process. Prity looked shell shocked and unsurprisingly remained speechless. She had just had her dignity stripped from her forever and there was no turning the clock back now. My stomach sickeningly churned for her as she sat there shaking.

'That was just what the quack ordered,' he cackled standing to his feet and wiping the sweat from his face. Prity got up and ran off past him and straight into the toilet where she slammed the door shut behind her, locking it immediately.

The thug then ripped off the tape from my mouth, taking with it some of the bum fluff that I had devoutly collected form my upper lip.

My blubbing continued, 'I...I...thought we had a deal. You get the money and leave us alone,' I said down cast and beaten.

'I don't see any deal chum. No contract and no agreement. I just get what I want that is the truth. The best thing about all of this is to watch your expression, I mean dude that is just so hilarious.'

Dalj had his head tucked down into his knees where he sat leaning against the wall next to me. He had remained in that position all throughout the ordeal, secretly praying for the madness to stop.

'Okay, it is time for the main course. The part that I have been waiting for the most and to draw a line under this saga,' he threatened with baleful barbarism.

What did he mean? Surely, I had fed the beast enough entertainment to satiate his sadistic cravings, but it seemed that it was not enough. It only meant one thing and now that he had his bit of fun, it was time for him to leave but not before expunging the only witnesses to his heinous crimes. As they say, dead men tell no tales...

Chapter 21

There is no sacrifice

What do you think about before you die? Where do you go when you die? I took a moment to contemplate these very facts in the sanctum of my mind. The answers remained only a discharging bullet away.

'Go on then beg for you gutless life back. Convince me why I should not just plug you and these followers right here and now,' he warned.

I had for the time it took the figurative board to revolve to seduce him with my trouser leg grabbing mercy for my ephemeral life on Earth. It was indeed a Hamlet moment and the next sixty seconds or so stood between my survival and that of being buried under a mountain of dirt six foot under.

I composed my inner thoughts quickly and assessed that no amount of pleading and grovelling was going to free me from the inevitable outcome today and flush me away from this depressive catacomb of pain that I had been held prisoner. I was already on the stake and the flames were just gently licking the sides of my face, moments away from turning me into smouldering ashes.

I took comfort with the fact that I had at least fulfilled my dream of making it in Bollywood when the opportunity came knocking and that was edifying in itself.

I looked up at Anil and then at the thug, they mocked me, to them I was nothing but a piece of scrunched up innocence, a sickening scrum of self pity and defiance.

All my life I had been knocked about by life's tests and tribulations. The many sacrifices that I had made had all been purposeless. Where had it got me? They say that if you keep your head down and live an honourable life then karma would always come up trumps for you. This was the talk of fools, because here I was like the Wicker Man, trapped in my own grave and with as much chance of escaping as getting an elephant through a cat flap. I felt sorry for Prity who had all the while remained in the bathroom no doubt crying her eyes out and praying for the vermin to leave us alone.

I felt her pain but there was nothing I could do to assist her, all I wanted to do was place a comforting arm around her shoulder and tell her that it was going to be okay.

I remembered that the Swami had told me that if I was to be successful then I was to ensure that I survived this day no matter what, and then I would have the pick of the fruit in the orchard. This feat was proving to be virtually impossible with the nose of a Magnum pointing so menacingly at me.

'Nothing to say, then get prepared for surprise number one.'

His eyebrows furrowed and a dark and vindictive hue cut across his face. He was seriously going to kill me. I struggled to break free from the chair but once again the thug held me down with a firm grasp of my shoulder.

'NO! STOP! I shouted. They were to be my last words. It was surreal and everything happened in slow motion, from my last desperate look in the face of the evil so personified standing before me to the clicking of the gun and the flash. I closed my eyes and it was over...

I felt no pain, just the trickling of blood where he stuck one straight through my heart. My body had gone into shock, his aim had been perfect and clinical. It was strange that I felt no immediate pain, just a hollow feeling followed by a coat of warmth spreading throughout my body. The blood continued to pour as I slowly opened my eyes to survey his handiwork, still feeling no pain at all. Maybe I was made of sterner stuff then I had given myself credit for.

I looked down at my chest and there it was the liquid seeping like a waterfall and down into my lap. I looked up at Anil and the thug and they stood there laughing like hyenas. He pressed the trigger again and then the penny dropped. It was a sophisticated water pistol and the second squirt of water in my face confirmed this sorry fact to me. There had been no blood and no shot into the heart, it was all pretence to scare the living daylights out of me and watch me whimper and plead for my life. It had all been a game of muscle flexing from this toothless, inbred hick.

He played me like a set of bongo drums and the egg yolk remained super glued to my chagrined face.

'Did you book our tickets?' he asked the thug.

'Yeah, two tickets all done,' confirmed the monster.

'Who are you? I shook my head asking the thug.

'He is a local network I have here in India and one that I will certainly be doing business with again after he sees what fee he will be paid for this assignment.'

The thug grinned back at me looking pleased with himself.

'Now, Sam you have had the starter, are you ready for the main meal and the next surprise?' he mocked.

Anil stepped forward, close enough for me to look up his flaring nostrils. He sniffed hard and then slipped on what looked like a knuckle duster from within his jean pocket with an element of decree. I was cornered and could do nothing, I closed my eyes and decided to take my beating like a man.

I sensed his gimlet eye balled temper had seized control of his senses as I had seen in the past. I lowered my head emitting a whining noise knowing what was about to arrive on my doorstep. My whining held no water as the wildcat drove a succession of heavy rib cracking punches into my mid section. The grooves of the knuckle duster sank neatly in-between my ribs. The pain making me wince and writhe as though I was being fried on an electric chair. BANG! BANG! The avalanche of hurt smashed through my core repetitively. There was no respite and my lungs took the battering full steam ahead. The distant screams of Dalj simply faded away into the background against my soul destroying turmoil. So, this is what it is like before you die, hissed my inner demon. I coughed up some blood, hoping that the sight of my claret would deter the aggressor from taking more than my dignity on this black day.

He was not impressed and slapped me across the face a number of times, each time harder and harder, hoping and praying to draw blood from my features. I caught a blurry glimpse of the crazed animal in full flight and smelt his ferocity pouring out of every god forsaken orifice as he carried on shamelessly raping my dignity as a man. He did not care if he left me for dead in the seat as he had some serious pent up anger that he felt more than comfortable unleashing on his captive victim. I went to plead, opening my mouth - SMASH! He knocked a tooth clean out of its socket, with a short spray of blood spurting on his demonic face. My heart cried for mercy for token mercy just this one time. BANG! He head butted me with full force knocking my head back violently. My eyes filled with a combination of water, blood and ingrained hatred, but I knew that it was now all over.

Right at that moment he suddenly stopped as the bathroom door opened and out stepped Prity. It was a bell saving moment and I opened my eyes painfully to see my baby girl in the flesh, perhaps this final time. She was a sight to behold, and in this moment akin to serendipitous smelling salts that my nostrils craved for like a junkie seeking out some heroin. She was dolled up, sexy and looking as scrumptious as I had ever seen her. Her face glowing and fresh and not what I expected to be confronted with especially after she had been brutally raped, oh…wait a bloody minute, I groaned loudly. The mist from my eyes cleared and I alarmingly realised the greatest trick ever to have been played on someone had just been acted out on me, hook, line and nose bloodied sinker.

Prity walked over to Anil and then in a moment that felt like a juggernaut had fallen on my chest she grabbed him by the back of the head and kissed him hard on the lips as though to say 'fuck you' to me and to make up for lost time between these sadistic and duplicitous lovers.

She let go off his head and turned to look at me smugly. Anil placed his hand on her bum, a place where it had been on many occasions whilst she was 'courting' me.

'And that my loser friend is the next surprise and check mate,' he barked triumphantly standing next to his trophy girl.

I sat in stunned silence, my face and body throbbing, my heart shattering into the tiniest of fragments. How could anyone be so downright evil? It meant that she had played me all the way through our relationship just to set me up so that she could steal my money with her long standing lover.

They had executed their plan with defining accuracy and I did not have any idea of such cunning planning on their part. Dalj looked just as mortified as me and actually shed some tears from where he sat, the tenets of a staunch friend. Suddenly and thankfully like a miracle I could see that Pinto was beginning to come out of her unconscious state and was slowly propping herself up against the wall near where she was laying. She was alive and kicking much to my obvious delight. Once she had regained a semblance of clarity with her surroundings she too looked aghast when she saw Prity caressing and stoking Anil a few feet away from her. She remained sat on the floor when she saw the gun/water pistol that Anil was still wielding. She announced her arrival back in the land of the living mumbling, 'Chal kum kar bhanchod, saala kutay da putt,' under her breath loud enough for Anil to raise his eyebrows at her. It was small consolation because the damage had been done.

I had a torrent of interrogative questions for the sneaky pair before they set off to walk out of the door and into the sunset and in a last ditch effort shouted, 'Just tell me why?' whilst spitting out a mouthful of blood to the floor beside me.

Prity stepped forward and let me have both barrels of uncensored ammunition. This was when I discovered what the words deceit and betrayal really meant...

Chapter 22

I can't believe it's not butter

Prity spoke to me like a piece of dirt on her shoe, 'Look, do you really think someone like me would be interested in a loser like you. It is not all about the fame and pursuing stupid dreams, it is all about getting rich or to die trying you understand now?'

Her hostile and bigoted outpouring left me under no illusions of the bile she felt towards me, when all I had ever done was cared for and loved her.

'So, everything we shared together, was it all a sham, a cover up?' I asked her cutting to the chase.

'Look, honey, you are a sweet guy and all that but for one I would never marry a gora (white guy), and you just haven't got that bit of flavour or bite that I am looking for in my man.'

Bite, was she kidding me? I would have bitten her effing nose off given half the chance.

'What about when you cried and stuff? When I saw you being held against your will in the room by the kitchen? The phone-call to Visperal? What did it all mean?'

I implored her to tell me the truth and justify every one of those occurrences.

I then braced myself to listen to more of her verbal diatribe.

'Did you really think that I didn't see you when you were jumping in and out of the shadows down by the corridor leading to the kitchen? We set you up, because after ten or so minutes we knew you would come looking for me like the budding blood hound you are, being all caring and weak like you displayed down to a tee.'

I shook my head in horrific disappointment. Her betrayal was executed sublimely and on a grandeur scale. She was a cold and calculating bitch who deserved every bit of her blood money. Anil stood by making small talk with his thug friend whilst I crossed verbal swords with Prity angling to get to the bottom of her callous culling of my trust in her.

'Oh and as for Baldip, that sucker was just cannon fodder for me. I am the one who put the telephone numbers of Anil and Terry in his phone. I mean come on, that was hardly the most conjuring trick to pull on someone like you. At times, you had that mushy love shit pouring out of your eyes, man it was suffocating. You are like a leech!'

There was simply no pause in her abusive stance towards me, she hurled tomato after tomato as I peered back at her pathetically in my personalised stock.

She had even framed Baldip for a crime that he didn't commit. The poor soul never saw the set up coming, and years of professional respect and reputation was scrunched up and pissed all over by the Indian Bonnie and Clyde. He had been sacked by me and stripped of his dignity in full view of Prity and the others that fateful day in the service station. He had been a mere pawn in the game of perfidy, and his feelings were traipsed all over by a herd of stampeding prevaricators. My heart went out to him and if only I could see him again to express my regret for mistrusting him so ostentatiously.

'Visperal? Did you phone him at the studio?' I felt like choking and the words stuck in my throat.

'No, no, you just don't get it do you. I never phoned him and to be frank I don't care two hoots about him, I never have. I am the one who should be getting an award or a role in a film for my acting. That was Anil who I was speaking to in the studio, we were setting up this final swansong for you here in this room.'

I had got it alright and studied her contorted features and wondered how I had let her sucker me so easily. It was as though I had been chomping on sucker sweets all throughout our time together and now the taste was back firing on me, my people-ometer had messed up big time.

'Come on we should go,' motioned Anil who was now getting agitated at Prity's insistence on putting me straight about our shambolic façade of a relationship.

'Wait, I need to get a few more things off my chest before I go,' insisted Prity.

Anil shrugged his shoulders and sat on the bed still holding the water pistol knowing that it was enough to prevent a demented but incognizant Pinto from sinking her denture gnashers into his neck.

'Think about when we met and how I bumped into you one day. Coincidence? Remember how I kept on apologising to you and how sorry you felt for me. Well, that was when it all started.'

The truth was skinning me alive but I wanted to hear more from the witch of Mumbai.

'We had already heard on the grapevine that you had all this money coming to you, thanks to Terry's big drunken mouth down in the boozer. He would brag all about you and tell anyone who would listen exactly how he would dupe you out of it when you reached eighteen. That was when Anil also got to hear about this, and together we hatched this plan to scam you out of it. Make sense now?'

I knew that some women could be nasty and vindictive but this was the ultimate coup of knockout blows, a genital crushing bag of deceit. When I had met her, she came across as the mild mannered and virginal girl who would not have said boo to a goose. The kind of lass who would weep at the end of mushy films, who would cower behind the sofa when watching a horror film, and to be brutally truthful, the kind of sweet filly that butter wouldn't melt in her innocent mouth. I had actually physically felt a sense of shared belonging with her. She had once been the colostrum, a critical life force in my haphazard existence, but now she had eclipsed the marker set by Judas with an act of calculated poison, one for which I could never forgive her.

'If I wanted a lap dog I would have bought one for Christmas. I have got all I need right here,' she pointed at the snake sat on the bed twirling his toy gun around his finger like John Wayne and he smiled back at her. The noose around my neck tightened a notch or two as she sniped at me again like a coiled snake.

'You were simply a crutch I utilised to get to this position and now you have expired your worth to me what do I need you for anyway?' She brought the hammer down with agonising brutality.

'The fake tears then, the hugs and those sweet intimate moments. You are telling me that it was all just one big act?' I don't know why I asked because the answer was sure to be an accompanying nail in my coffin but

I could not help myself and had gone past the point of no return with my sanity.

'Precisely, now you are getting it, finally. Swing the straw out of your head for a moment and look at you, and then look at me. Kind of like beauty and the beast don't you agree?'

The stroppy mop had made a dogs dinner out of me and kept landing a succession of low blows, a barrage of ghoulies swiping kicks, and all the time I sat there and absorbed her best shots. The battle had been won, but the war, well that was for another time I smirked wryly.

'The rape...why?' I asked, my innards twisted from the bombardment of my senses.

'That was Prity's idea. A great way to stick the final boot in I say. You are lucky because I just wanted to kill you, you sad mother fucker. Where are your parents anyway hey? Oh, yes they are strumming their little harps up on a cloud somewhere, diddums, get over it you whining cat or I will tear you a new arsehole.' Anil spat out the abuse without a shred of sympathy for my loved ones. It seemed that the jealous sky of envy hung over this day drawing the hungriest hounds from far afield to feast on my broken dreams and decimated carcass. I had just taken another heavy hit on mount despair and my mind was in freefall, I understood the hurt and anguish would last for a lifetime. The pain would one day haunt me in my quiet moments as a granddad rocking in my chair in some old people's home. There was no escaping this tangible torment that I had been dragged through by my hair.

I had come all this way to India to be stabbed in the back by one of my inner circle confidants and supposedly loyal girlfriend. I had then sadly sacked the one guy who was there only to help me. I had also seen Pinto upping her loony tunes yard stick a few bars higher and almost coming a cropper in several lip biting moments. I had fought off the continual presence of Spiros in his quest to be king pin and had managed to hoodwink Terry and Myleene with a chess move that Karpov would have given me a standing ovation for. I had even managed to evade the grasping clutches of Anil up until this prophetic day, and now all I had to show for my gusto was a return trip to Film City later and that was about it.

Like, I said at the start of this story, money truly is the root of all evil and changes the most resolute of people into greedy, mutinous and manipulative dip weeds. Prity and Anil were no different to many individuals out there, thirsty and always seeking out the next way to make a quick buck no matter who they trampled over to get it. This was the fabric of today's society depicted in such transparency.

My world had been snatched away from me and the culprits were flipping the bird at me with both hands, chalking me up on the floor of the hotel room before exiting. I remained wistful as Prity scooped up her belongings, mainly her cosmetics on the bed.

'Sorry about the mess darling, I guess I had to make it all authentic just for the crack. I will buy you some new stuff once we get out of here.' Anil slithered up with his words to my deserting queen.

'Sam, one more thing to ponder, that day when you went out gallivanting in the forest to see some prophet guy, well what do you think Prity was doing when you were gone? Hmm, I remember the session vividly, and in your bed. Just think when you were speaking to her that evening she still had my juice sloshing in her crack, nice eh?'

Prity looked at him disapprovingly. Even that remark was far too graphic for her delicate ears and she shook her head clearly incensed at his intimation that she was a piece of meat that he spoke of in such fashion.

His depravity was disgusting and I felt the knife twist a full three hundred and sixty degree angle, completely disembowelling me with his acidic details.

'Prity, the time when I saw your parents, was that all fake too?' I whined bracing myself for the inevitable and crucifying truth to be rammed down my throat with a sharp stiletto.

Once she had put her bag together, she turned to me for a final time and chirped, 'Yes, it was just business Sam, remember that. You will learn one day not to be so trusting, think of it as an experience.'

Oh well, thanks for the tip sweetheart but I think I will hang on to that thought when I tie myself to some heavy chains and throw myself off the nearest bridge after seeing my life go down the plug hole along with my self respect, credibility and nose hairs.

'Come on we have a plane to catch,' urged an increasingly annoyed Anil.

'Oh and just remember one thing if you forget everything else, if you try and follow us you are dead, if you try and call the police, you are dead and finally if you even look at us wrong in the future, guess what, ahh yes you are fucking DEAD MEAT!!' He shouted the last part causing Pinto to jump out of her wrinkly skin and Dalj to screw his face up in pure fear. It had worked and I knew that it was the last thing that I wanted to do, they had won, and there was no recourse.

Then the orchestrators of my sudden fall from grace walked out, never to be seen again. I had been schooled. The saloon doors flapped wildly with the gun slinging bandits clutching the loot and waltzing off to soak up the rays on some paradise island at my expense.

Pinto staggered to her feet and started to untie us one by one. This took her over ten minutes and when she had finished Dalj placed his hand on my shoulder and pulled me in close for a man to man hug. It was what I needed in this moment of extremis. I hugged back even though my body ached and throbbed from the beating I had just taken. Even Pinto joined in for some love, hugging the pair of us as though we were her long lost sons. We stayed there entwined for a minute and then two minutes, when I became increasingly uncomfortable, so pulled away slowly with the inadvertent drool from Pinto's mouth soaking my shoulder. She couldn't help herself and it appeared was hugely overcome by the emotions that were free flowing in the group hug, and needless to say thankful to be alive in the circumstances.

The pump and adrenaline of the situation along with the lingering stench of treachery fused together caused me to repeatedly cough and splutter for a good few minutes. Life was cheap and I held the towel firmly in my hand in readiness to toss it into the ring for the final time and end this saga for good, but something stopped me as another twisting fork on this perilous road could be seen shimmering in the distant and dusty plains ahead of me. There was still one more roll of the dice, one more poker hand to play before that towel went hurtling to the centre of the ring...

Chapter 23

Lucidity and veracity –
brother's in arms

'We are so stupid and gullible. How could we have let ourselves be taken in by them? Schoolboy errors and plain betrayal, that's what this is all about. What has the world come to hey?' Dalj summed up the feelings of the group expertly.

He was right, only a fool would have let them take every lasting memory of one's life in the manner they did. Here I was in a foreign country with the world at my feet a few minutes ago and now I didn't even have a pot to piss in with my ex girlfriend or ex acquaintance being more apt running off into the wilderness with my arch enemy. They could have written a book about this purgatory – that was no mistake.

Pinto sat rocking on the bed and muttering Punjabi profanities to herself. She may have been old and slightly senile but she certainly knew the gravity of the situation as her rocking became more and more intense, finally and over zealously she rocked too far and went tumbling over the other side of the bed. Dalj rescued her once again and we sat and colluded for the next few moments. 'There has to be something we can do?' asked Dalj.

I rubbed my hands together and took some deep breaths. I had time to reflect and make sense of it all. I used a wet wipe to touch up the worst bits of my face where he had struck me, and couldn't help but prod my tongue into the gaping hole that had been left by my one of my molars.

'Why didn't I see through that bitch? I am so foolish. I would rip her heart out if ever I saw her in Slough, I am telling you mate I will not be responsible for what I do to her. If she has any brain cells, she would do well to move out with her gangster boyfriend or I will make it my mission in life to catch up with her.' Dalj spoke directly from his heart and you can't shoot a guy for that. His whole attitude and response to the fiasco was laudable and he was assured of my hand in friendship for as long as he lived.

'But I thank God that it is all over now and we can get back to our normal lives,' his words conveyed the struggle and emotions of a doleful son of the desert, but as for the game being over, I wrestled with other contradictory thoughts.

Dalj and Pinto sat on the bed in contemplative thought with the grinding of the cogs in all our heads churning and the crunching of straw in Pinto's case.

In the meantime I collected my belongings, heavy hearted but with purpose. Once the suitcase was zipped up and secured. I picked up my mobile phone and hit the redial button. Dalj looked on quizzically. Even Pinto's ears pricked up in anticipation. Dalj turned to Pinto and said that I was calling a taxi to take us to a restaurant for some food as we had booked on to the later flight, one that was departing a few hours after the pair of Machiavellian con artists.

I pressed the mobile to my ear when I heard the dialling tone on the other end of the phone, and waited patiently for the recipient to answer. Dalj meanwhile flicked open his mobile phone and began to play one of the many classic Hunterz tracks, in this case it was 'Hare Hare,' a truly legendary song and this even had me tapping my foot whilst I stood nearby. This was the perfect aphrodisiac for all of us and helped ease the suffering we had been exposed to on this day of jumbled up emotions. I felt as though I had been fed with one hand and slapped with another, my pensive ambivalence was short lived when a voice responded on the phone. The soothing tones of Hunterz playing loudly in the background meanwhile lifted my sultry and moody face and I told the person on the other end of the phone to make their way to the hotel, pronto. I put the phone back in my pocket and waited, propping myself up against the TV table listening and allowing my spirit to be carried away with the next Hunterz tune, 'Rehle Rehle,' yet another masterpiece of ear magic. Once again, the timing of the song was impeccable and I indulged with mind, body and soul as the track belted out of Dalj's mobile phone.

We waited for half an hour in the hotel room that had become a dungeon of chicanery for me, it felt like the walls were slowly caving in. I looked at my watch and then again.

'What are we waiting for mate, a taxi?' Dalj's innocence was intoxicating if not irritating at this moment. I was scheming and needed time to manifest my thoughts before acting. Then there was a knock on the door. I smiled at the others and walked over slowly. Who had I summoned in this hour of need? Dalj and Pinto looked on in curious anticipation. I opened the door and extended my arms out hugging the guest with a heartfelt and meaningful embrace. The mystery stranger reciprocated and I heard gasps from Dalj and 'Hai hai, nee ma murjimaa' from Pinto whilst she simultaneously banged her palm against her forehead several times in quick succession. This was a common Asian trait that I had witnessed in many Bollywood movies and through the extended family activities that Dalj would often invite me on. Translated it means – hai hai where shall I die. An interesting poser given the circumstances I mused.

I had summoned my good friend and inner circle companion Baldip to the party. Dalj stood up and shook his hand and Pinto waved from her position having calmed down from her initial knee jerk reaction.

Baldip walked in and stood by the bathroom door, he looked serious, and without a skip of the heartbeat, I settled down into business. There was some much needed clarification needed so that everyone realised exactly what was going on and what was going to happen.

'Firstly, thanks for coming when I needed you most, I appreciate what you have done for me up until now.' I welcomed Baldip back and regained his confidence with my allies.

'I need you to take me to the airport one last time because there is something I need to do. It is risky and it may back fire on me but I need your trust and understanding as a group to help me do what I need to do.' I searched their faces for approval for this final mission of mine, but none was forthcoming, instead there were looks of resignation and disfavour.

Don't get me wrong I would have rather have shaved my shaved my head with a cheese grater than return to the pit of terror but this was something that I had to do. It was my time to live the life of a lion and not a lamb.

Dalj especially seemed astounded that I had the temerity to suggest that we jump back in the frying pan after the narrowest of escapes from the madman and his thug accomplice.

I had to calm him down after he stood up and kicked the chair over, and banged the table with his fist.

'You had better tell me you are joking, right? There is no way I am going to expose myself to any more danger now that we have escaped with our lives intact.' He was vociferous in his opinion and had disconcertingly changed his tune from only moments before when he had talked about stalking the earth searching for them and virtually crucifying them if they crossed his path. Now, this cat had altered his approach to the problem when there was a sniff of meeting them again, maybe he was scared, and I totally understood his ever weakening plight.

I attempted to reassure him but to no avail with Pinto chipping in and siding with her grandson. She removed my arm from around his shoulder and cast me a look of indignation and disapproval. They were disgusted that I was even contemplating trying to end the day with a meaningless pyrrhic victory of sorts. (A pyrrhic victory means to win a battle, but at the expense of substantial losses on your side. It was named after the great Emperor Pyrrhus of Epirus).

They did not understand that there were a couple of loose ends that needed tying, and if I missed this opportunity then yet another battle would have been won by the axis of evil. It was token redemption and I desperately sought their support one last time. I was like a boxer on one knee in the heavyweight championship bout and had the referee breathing down my neck with the one to ten count, now reaching six. I just needed my corner to give me the final push, the last strands of encouragement to pull myself up off the ground, to cut through the jungle of fatigue and worthlessness to go another three minutes, that is all I asked for. Right now, Dalj was standing there signalling the end and being a stellar friend.

'Just come with me please I beg you, I need to get something off my chest and then I promise we will go. I tried once more to tap into their good natures and supplicated them for their comprehension.

Pinto not one to say much started the remonstrations by saying, 'He is madman, you not listen,' she prodded Dalj in the chest with her haggard finger.

'Why can't you just let it go mate, what is so important that you need to confront them? What is it that you could not have said to them when they were here? Did the cat have your tongue then or what?'

His unwelcomed but understandable depredation was unsettling in my hour of need.

'I will explain everything to you, but we are running out of time, they board the flight in less than two hours, we must go now. I kept chipping away at him, chiselling my way through his resolve. It was working and he appeared to lighten up, sensing that there had to be a damn good reason for me to want to commit hari kari at the airport.

'Look we are not going you stupid arsehole. You have to realise when you have been beaten,' he shouted whilst waving his hand across my face clipping my nose as he did so. I reeled back and was now beginning to lose my sense of humour with him. Why wouldn't he listen to me?

'What's the matter with him? He will end up getting seriously hurt if he goes, that is for sure,' he spluttered sitting down on the bed again having let me know the veracity of his feelings.

'I will not let you do it mate, you will have to get past me first because it will be one of those mistakes you will rue when you are older and you are drinking soup out of a straw with your prosthetic limb. It is a suicide mission, you heard what he said, he will kill you.' Dalj rubber stamped his disapproval in blood and that was that.

Baldip looked at me with heavy eyes and looked embarrassed to have been caught in the cross fire of the domestic that had kicked off in front of him, but to his credit he remained an impartial bystander.

'What about Terry and Myleene? Don't you think they are still looking for you? What if they are at the airport too? This has got indiscriminate massacre written all over it like a bad rash and I am not fucking happy about it, not happy at all,' he shot his bile filled and unfettered load at me.

I had heard enough and like a trained mercenary, my mind was already made up. The sword was forged, and I was going with or without them - however the chips fell. I locked myself in the bathroom and splashed some much needed water on my face. The sensation was amazing and I felt the water taking away the lashings of abuse I had been subjected to, I splashed over and over until I could finally look at myself in the mirror with any kind of dignity. I looked at my face for a few moments studying every contour of my bruised and battered mug, looking for signs of a broken man, but instead I saw one ready for one more round.

In life that is sometimes all you need to do when the chips are down, when everything around you is crumbling, you just need to suck it all in and go that one more round, because that is the round that makes all the difference between winning and losing, success and failure.

Suddenly a ghostly apparition appeared in the reflection in the mirror. It was my father, and in the general chaos of the day, his timing was crucial as I was about to embark upon the final but most deadly mission of them all.

'Father, what do I do? I am confused!' I poured my heart out to the spirit hovering in the reflection behind me. It was at times like these that I wished that I could have just reached over and tightly hugged him. I missed him, his smell, his presence and for what he stood for. I started to cry.

'Son, you need to do it. Take this final step and close the chapter and then move on. Don't let anyone stand in you way, it is what your mother wants too.'

I lifted my eyebrows,' Mum, does she see what is happening? I asked, the tears streaming like waterfalls down my face and splashing with thunderous aplomb on the white basin where I had now rested my hands.

'She tells me every day how much she loves you, she always watches over you as I do. Now go and finish it son, go and say your piece and we can all rest. Good luck! And, well done, we are both so proud of you. We love you son, we both love you so much…'

With that he disappeared into the air leaving me standing there, lip trembling, and hands shaking. My body felt weak and the experience of such a hive of activity was slowly slurping the juice from my bones. They say that experience is the hardest teacher, at first it gives you the test and then the lesson, I felt that experience was about ten nil up on the score board, but I still had a little time...

I opened the door and Dalj practically fell though into the bathroom, minus the plastic cup and listening device, landing on a scrunched up heap on the floor. He looked a trifle embarrassed and quickly regained his footing and dusted his arms down. He had been ear wigging outside after he had heard the voices within.

'Err, who were you talking to in there mate? Your mobile is on the table over there.' He looked puzzled.

'Don't worry you wouldn't believe me if I told you,' I brushed past him and retrieved my mobile from the table.

'You been crying? he asked supportively.

'Nah, it is only water hey,' I bluffed well.

'Was that your dad you were talking to?' His voice was full of sincerity. I looked at him and there was nothing more to say.

'I am going to face my fear, face my demons, are you with me?' I said standing by the door ready to leave with Baldip.

'Of course we are. We came together and we will go together, even if it means that it all ends today, then you have our support.'

I smiled and thanked them for their support and we then checked out of the hotel whilst Baldip saddled up the minibus with our cases. Within moments we were on the tarmac and heading off towards a certain bloodbath at The Chattrapathi Shivaji International Airport. It was here that destiny would either have the last laugh with its puppets or an even more forbidding and ominous programme for its victims. One thing was guaranteed - there would be a definite bloodbath, and I was the inane culprit responsible for taking my friends to their certain doom. That was a bitter and repentant burden on my soul, but now there was no turning back as the pendulum of death swung with deadly perversity towards us...

Chapter 24

Pincer movement

The journey to the airport was not without incident with Pinto letting rip a few broccoli laced farts that almost gassed us all to within one inch of our lives. At one stage, I was not even sure that I would make it to the airport to say my piece such was the donkey kicking power her farts carried. She was the secret grand master of flatulence and we faced the death of a thousand farts being in such a confined space.

'Just one more, one more and I am going to swing for her,' yelled an irate Dalj, who I was having trouble restraining from my position at the front of the car. He was moments away from strangling Pinto as she went to lift one of her bum cheeks up again for the knock out blow. Thankfully, I managed to stop her on this occasion and quickly opened all the windows. Dalj sucked the Mumbai air like a hoover with his head hovering out of the window. After a few difficult moments, parity was restored and the arduous journey continued without further ado.

'How did you got to the hotel so quick?' Dalj probed Baldip whilst we plodded onwards.

Dalj was not sitting comfortably and was radiating an aura of disquiet. He communicated with Baldip searching deep into the pair of eye sockets that stared back at him unblinking through the rear view mirror in his seated position behind the driver. The spotlight was flicked on and the interrogation was only just warming up.

'I never left,' replied Baldip looking at me first and then scrutinising Dalj's face for his reaction through the rear view mirror.

'You mean you were at the hotel all this time?' enquired Dalj, hanging on like a dog with a bone.

'Yes that is correct. I booked myself in another room on the day I was sacked,' he responded quick as a flash. I glanced back and noticed the pained expression displayed on Dalj's face. He was trying to piece together the information and clues he had, but all I could see were the multitude of question marks circling above his head and repetitive Family Fortunes 'Uh Uhs,' slapping him back down to square one at every turn.

'So you were at the hotel, but why?' This was indeed the sixty four million dollar question.

Baldip remained impassive, concentrating on the road and occasionally flicking his eyes across at me and then at Dalj in the mirror.

'Oh, I see so that was your minibus at the hotel that day, I knew it.' Dalj was in sizzling form and at this rate would have single handily solved all the world's long standing mysteries.

I turned back and nodded approvingly. It was commendable that Dalj was allowing his brain to remain tirelessly concentrated on the sign posted signals that pieced together a lot more than met the naked eye. It was better he done this than wallow in self deprecation. They say that the definition of honesty is not holding back the pertinent details, and right now I had to stop the unnecessary questioning, it was not the time and place for such lunacy, and instead I needed resolute focus for the task we were foisting ourselves into, or otherwise it was all but over.

By now, Pinto was merrily hurtling around in a carriage of slumber somewhere in the clouds, her closed eyes and flip top expression on the top of the rear seats was a bit of a give away.

'What about Terry and Myleene?' he added, his brain engaging quicker than his mouth, and unresponsive to my attempts to cajole him to maintain his focus.

'They are dead!' Baldip's response was unrepentant. This modest and unassuming man was a trained killer. Is that what this was all about? Dalj's sudden respect for the driver had floated off like a bloated behemoth into the abyss, and if I knew Dalj as I did, I could tell that he was having kittens even being in the same car as the mercenary before him.

'D...d...dead,' he stuttered incredulously.

'To the world mate, Baldip had already told me.' I enlightened Dalj with this startling revelation.

As the darkest and most well guarded secrets of the trip to Mumbai were slowly unravelling, I sensed a pervading atmosphere of fear and even more anguish caking the interior of the minibus we were being conveyed in.

'Did you kill them?' asked a rattled Dalj, hoping that it was all a big mistake and that he had misheard him.

'No! No! I am a family man,' said Baldip, 'I just heard from talking to the hotel staff. The barman was suspicious about guests being drugged and taken up to their rooms and called in the police because he said that the gang was still on the premises. My brother works in the police, and they arrived in the early hours of the morning and stumbled across the pair as they tried to escape in the reception.'

Dalj's ears pricked up and he lapped up every word.

'All they had to do was hand themselves in and it would have been a couple of quick arrests, but they insisted on fighting back after a bottle of poison was found on them. Despite warnings, they armed themselves with smashed beer glasses from the bar. Two shots later and they both perished. It was so unavoidable,' I addressed the incident matter of fact.

'Baldip knew all this information because he had been staying at the hotel and he was fully aware of the people who were trying to harm me.' I added, sucking what little life force Dalj had out of his body.

Baldip had already briefed me about this before, and I said a quick prayer for the fallen victims. Despite the ties I had with them, it was surreal for I felt no other emotion, just one of detachment and freedom. I did not shed a tear for them and took solace with the thought that karma had dished out its justice for years of abuse and victimisation that I suffered at the hands of their spineless existence.

Dalj looked like a human Martini, shaken and stirred, but quietly accepted their fate.

'Mate, what about that stuff about Spiros on the beach with Baldip. I thought you said that was dodgy?' Anil would not let go with a continual slew of questions coming in thick and fast.

'Again, Baldip confessed to me that Spiros was trying to bribe him to get the part in the film, that is all that was,' I exclaimed.

'How do you know all this?' he said pointing the finger of suspicion at my head.

'After the beach that day I had a long chat with Baldip where we discussed everything and I mean everything,' this insight spoke volumes under his scrutiny.

'The phone-calls at breakfast then, surely that was not business,' screamed Dalj, desperately seeking a chink in Baldip's disconcerting behaviour.

'No, you are right that was not business. That was his wife complaining that he was not spending enough time at home,' I added batting away another of his accusative balls.

Dalj sank back in his seat and the interrogation and tidal wave of questions momentarily slaked, whilst he pieced together the jumbled up fragments in his head.

Approximately ten minutes later the silence was again broken, 'So, why are we going to the airport then? What is so important? I get it! The money is fake? Is that what it is?' asked Dalj sounding as though he had cracked the case. He was like the Terminator and kept on coming, gnawing away at my trouser leg like a diseased and rabid dog.

'No the money is definitely real. I took it out that day when we came back from the Swami remember?' I dashed his line of investigation with my swift riposte.

'Oh, so why are we going again?' he foraged for some light to be shed.

'Wait a few more minutes and you will see,' I said reassuringly.

'What about Spiros? Is he really gone just like that?' asked Dalj curiously.

'I am confident, he knows when he is beaten,' I said emphatically but not one hundred per cent certain that

I was not walking in on a deadly conspiracy of some description.

The next few moments drifted by silently while Dalj inserted some new batteries in his voice box and let the hamster running the cogs in his head out of his wheel to stretch his legs and get some oxygen.

'Have you called your brother?' I asked Baldip.

'He is waiting for us at the airport,' he replied confidently.

We pulled into the airport car park and at that moment my guts churned with queasy and nauseating despoil. My body began to shake from the trickle of adrenaline that began to shuttle through my blood stream. I had reached the point of no return and I must admit I was petrified about coming face to face with the people who had served me up like a Foie Gras duck on a platter. I stepped out of the vehicle, my legs like jelly and wobbling uncontrollably. This was the time to get out of the sandbox and on the stage for my swansong performance, to stop being a cheer leader and growing up into a super star. I sucked in the night air and headed off to the terminal entrance, I knew that Anil was capable of killing and right now I was covered in meat paste and going into the lions den…

Chapter 25

The final resolution

We entered the airport terminal and quickly made our way to the TV monitors depicting the departures in the next few hours. There it was the flight to London, scheduled to leave in approximately one and a half hours. Baldip beckoned us to follow him as he knew exactly where the duo would be hanging out before departing the country. We duly followed him up various escalators and pathways all the while trying to suppress the increasing apprehension and anxiety that filled my lungs like death fuel.

We searched with fervour, in this lounge and that lounge but to no avail. Despite the relentless and frantic surge of exploration from all of us we were drawing blanks. This included a groggy Pinto, who was being effectively carried by us, yawning repeatedly like the Lion bar advert, after she had been rudely woken up from her forty winks by Dalj screaming 'fire in the hole bibi, wake up,' at the top of his voice.

I was giving up any hope of catching them with every proverbial stone unturned. It gripped my shit that they had fled and denied me one last menial meeting.

Baldip looked at me and then at his watch, he looked as perplexed as I did. I asked Dalj if he had any joy when he returned from checking out an adjacent lounge to where we were standing, and he replied with a monosyllabic grunt. This was a tell tale sign that his body was now firmly ensconced in the fight or flight mode due to the severity of what was at stake if we found our quarry.

Just when I was giving up any hope, I glanced up casually in the distance and my eyes widened. I had the money shot, my eagle eyes had spotted them with the National Lottery arrow pointing down from the sky screaming *'it's you.'* They had not seen us as yet, as they sat in a restaurant cubicle pecking at some snacks on a plate. I nudged the others and then began to take the first few tentative steps in their direction. I had the element of surprise on my side and this was a consoling factor the closer I reached the pair watching them frolicking like two rabbits in their love hutch.

The nearer I got to them, the more I could taste the sweet embrace of death in my spit. The more I discovered several chinks in my own armour that I did not realise existed until this moment, including my inability to disguise my nerves when confronted with a life or death situation such as the one I was weltering in, or the way my body forged on despite knowing the outcome would be sticky to say the least.

Several feet away from them and still they gazed lovingly into each-others eyes like a couple of love struck puppies. There was a storm coming their way, and they had not battened down the hatches.

I surveyed the territory they occupied, there were knives and forks on the table, there was mustard capable of being thrown into one's eye, and there was the fist fighting capabilities of Anil, a freakishly strong bruiser whose force I had already felt. If I got this wrong then I would have been 'keema.'

Strangely enough when I was a mere hair grabbing distance from them, I briefly looked back and Baldip, Dalj and even Pinto were standing several metres behind me. Their pitter patter fairy steps had worked with skilful cunning, and as if by some miracle, they were suddenly not next to me when the sparks would invariably fly. Well I guess, would you want to rattle the cage of a known killer?

Suddenly Anil stood up and pushed past the table confronting me at the entrance to the restaurant. He moved fast and had already encroached my personal zone with a blink of the eye. He pranced around screaming,' What the fuck do you want now? Was my beating not enough? I thought I made myself clear to you!' he hissed menacingly, spraying me with spittle from the foam that started to appear on the sides of his mouth.

Then just like the Rocky films, there were camera flashes of Pinto shouting, 'Bachke raaaaayyooooooo.' Dalj screaming, 'Watch out Sammmmmmmm.' Baldip shouting,'Noooooooooo!'

These screams and Anil's predictable reaction was the necessary kick in the pants jolt that I needed and transmogrified me from a bag of jangling nerves to a galvanised and assured presence. I had snapped into action like a defibrillator machine thanks solely to this injection of acid from my arch enemy.

I noticed that a crowd was already gathering behind me and the other diners in the restaurant were tuned in with popcorn, 3d glasses, and camera phones at the ready.

Prity looked nervous at the thought of my entourage

and me turning up to piss all over her firework display, but it was tough, I was here on business and right now I had my audience and my cue to start.

I looked past Anil and focussed on Prity as she sat in solitude at the table, 'Remember a while back I said that you should never under estimate me and when I mentioned to you that I was a good actor. Well guess what honey I knew about your scam all along.'

Anil stepped back open mouthed looking back at Prity. She shared the same goofy expression as her lover as the penny not so much dropped but came shattering down to the ground gutting them like fish.

Pinto came and stood beside me, her hands on her hips, on the other side of me Dalj stood with new found admiration for me and a chest puffing bravado that had fluctuated like a yo yo throughout the trip.

'You see that day when we left the beach, I poured my heart out to Baldip. I don't know why? I guess he looked like a trustworthy person and sometimes that is all you can rely on, just gut instinct. He really wanted to know what it took for me to be here and so I told him all about Terry, Myleene, you (I pointed at Anil as he listened carefully), and even the problems that I was having with Spiros.'

At this point Baldip appeared from the gathering onlookers filling up behind me and saddled up next to Pinto, he was my extra lung.

I continued, 'That was when he told me about Spiros trying to bribe him at the beach, but being a man of patriotism and dependability, he was not impressed with such an underhand approach and felt inclined to warn me about the ill conceived motives of Spiros. This was when I warmed to his honesty.'

Prity remained speechless and Anil had now sat down with the look of a wounded seal.

'During our stay I observed how you kept on denigrating Baldip's reputation and tried to bad mouth him at every opportunity. I knew you were only doing this so that you could get him out of the picture and you even had the audacity to dupe Dalj into telling me that Baldip was bad news too. You realised that Baldip would let me in on the conversation he had caught you having and so you got rid of him as swiftly as you could. It would have upset the months of planning wouldn't it?'

The executioners axe was resting on Prity's throat the further I delved into the events of the week.

'He had told me before in one of our many chats that he saw you whispering on the phone to Anil, telling him how much you loved him, couldn't wait to be with him, and how you were planning to dupe me out of my money with your lover.' I turned the thumb screws a notch more.

'Bad move, because Baldip here has grown up on the streets of Mumbai and can smell bullshit at fifty paces. He was not deceived when you said that it was your mum on the phone, and when he told me like the true friend he his, I realised the danger I was in from my supposed girlfriend.'

Someone in the crowd shouted, 'Crucify them,' it was a fellow Brit who was travelling home and was over whelmed by what he was hearing as were other strands of the crowd.

'I knew all about the set up in the room by the kitchen, it was too obvious. Every time you tried to plan a scam, I was one step ahead with the help of Baldip. Remember in the hotel room the little glances I would make up at the ceiling, well, it was my way of saying look how near you are to getting my money and fulfilling your sick dream, and so eat my shit. Even the service station was a great acting platform for Baldip and I. It was a chance to put you at ease and pretend that your sick scam was on track, clever eh?'

I circled the pair of them as they sat marooned on the table lost in the mystery of their demise.

'The greatest trick that I ever pulled was out acting you two morons. Years of watching Bollywood movies had paid dividends. I would look at you in our so called intimate moments and try to comprehend how you could have been so evil to try and do what you were doing to me. To make me actually believe that you had been raped beggars belief, but I guess that it doesn't quite have the requisite pizzazz it was supposed to now does it? Now you realise that I had seen through your entrapment and calculated ruse since Baldip let me into your murderous secret.'

'Ahh, that is why I caught him smirking over the last few days, he knew,' whispered Dalj to Baldip, who nodded agreeably.

I paused for a moment and took in some much needed breaths. The crowd was abuzz with whispers and tittle tattle, gasps and expressive sighing. It felt like the entire eyes of the airport were firmly fixated on the small group of us gathered in the gold fish bowl of the restaurant. No-one felt inclined to move us on or interfere with the kangaroo court, because like in gladiatorial times the blood thirsty crowd wanted more, they wanted heads on sticks, and to think that I was going to fly on a plane with some of these sadistic bastards, an interesting but yet frightening prospect in anyone's language.

'My father always told me to be one step ahead, to be street smart and to outfox those who were trying to outwit me. I listened and studied those words carefully. I even had a Swami telling me that there would be blood and to be careful of those around me who would try and take what I had, including my self esteem.'

Dalj nodded in agreement behind me, still snorting like a bull as more details emerged of the deceit.

'Until that day, when my dear friend Baldip had pointed the finger of suspicion at you, I had no idea that someone as beautiful and innocent as you could have schemed so deviously since the moment we met to steal my money. It just did not make sense to me.'

Anil started to get agitated and the blitzing ambush and element of surprise that I had counter attacked him with was losing its shine, 'Yeah, so what? You know all about us, what does it mean?' It doesn't change anything. You still got fucked player.'

'Carpe diem!,' I said calmly looking at Anil and then Prity deep into the sockets of their eyes, for now I owned their souls and they knew it. The pride of Slough was leaving his calling card.

'It means to seize the day and the moment. You son of a motherless pig,' I said to Anil clicking my fingers.

Right then a group of police officers waded through the crowd like a speedboat parting the waves, it was Baldip's brother and his platoon of able bodied officers, one or two no doubt with the blood of Terry and Myleene still fresh on the souls of their shoes.

Anil saw the net closing and suddenly jumped up from his seat picking up the steak knife and holding it to the throat of Prity, pulling her by the hair as he did so. She screamed from sheer disappointment if nothing else, trying to wrestle free from his vice like grip. Her struggles were futile and Anil dug the knife in a few inches deeper than he should have instantly drawing blood. The on-lookers gasped in horror as all eyes were squarely focussed on this rapidly developing hostage situation.

Anil's reaction was a clear statement that he did not fancy getting a visit in his Mumbai prison cell from a guy called Bubba holding a bar of soap in the early hours of the night.

Prity vomited a green alcoholic and slush type substance out of her mouth and down her top when she saw the stream of blood dripping down her neck, her body convulsing from the trauma that had suddenly shattered her idyllic get away. What a fall from grace for my former beauty queen I thought watching her vomiting over herself and having her throat slit from a back stabbing junkie boyfriend. They deserved one another as Anil continued to twirl Prity around by the hair whilst flashing the knife at anyone who dared stray into the combat arc around him.

'Please, let me go,' shrieked Prity, clearly overcome with imminent fear and loathing for Anil.

'Shut up you whore, or I will stick you,' he cut some more, scraping a piece of flesh from her neck as he did so.

'Drop the weapon or you will be shot,' barked the officer holding a gun directly to Anil's head pushing me to one side.

Anil gritted his teeth and growled back, he had the look of a possessed madman, it was the same look he had when he had beat me to within one inch of my life in the hotel room, a chance that I took and one that nearly backfired on me and cost me my life.

'Please Sam help me, please help me, I am sorry…' screamed Prity demoralised and forlorn.

Now she wanted my help, how the worm had turned. I shook my head, it was her grave and she was lying in it. I had stopped eating those sucker sweets a few days ago and now she was up to her neck in her own blood and despair with no-one but her greedy self to blame. If she died at the hands of her lover then it was a decision for the tentacles of karma to make, not a humble pawn like me.

'GET BACK! OR SHE DIES!' he yelled whilst pressing the blade up against her jugular again.

'DROP IT! DROP IT!' The officer next to me almost blew my ear drums out with his high pitched order.

'YYYAAAAHHHHHHHH,' Anil ditched Prity and ran towards us with the steak knife slashing wildly in a figure of eight in front of his body. He made it several feet before the sounds of five shots echoed around the airport and he was gunned down like a dog, drilled full of life ending lead. The shots scooped him off his feet and sent him crashing through the restaurant window shattering glass everywhere. The shards of glass scattered on to the tables and on the floor, embedding into most of the rubber neckers' who strayed close by to smell the blood dripping from Prity and thus creating a plethora of side shows where people had been hit with the glass. Amidst the banshee type wails form the on-lookers and mini ambulance rooms being set up, I saw Prity seize her opportunity to scarper from the scene hoping that no-one would realise that she had fled the crime scene in amongst the chaos that was developing.

She was wrong, and before I had a chance to sneeze Pinto darted past me in bare feet hopping over the dead motionless body of Anil, and expertly skipping over the fragments of glass like they were land mines. Out she sprinted, her chappals (sandals) in her hands and held like batons. Surely, Pinto was not a secret agent all this time I thought also giving chase behind her like a warped Benny Hill scene.

Prity was now at the escalators leaving a trail of claret in her wake, and thought she had all but made it. All the while she was being pursued by a heat seeking missile in the form of wrinkly Pinto who was now screaming at the top of her voice, 'Budooo, budooo.'

It was alarmingly confirmed at that moment that Pinto was no secret agent, but instead just a samosa or two short of a picnic, but this did not stop her, 'Budooooo, budoooooo,' she yelled gaining ground on Prity. Pinto, like a ball of fire blazed through the remaining gatherers reaching Prity at the foot of the escalator. There she unleashed the full dogs of war on her, spanking and striking her with chappals held in both hands. It was well known in the Asian circles that you didn't mess with a dadiji wielding chappals of mass destruction or the end was definitely nigh. Once she had unleashed those dogs from the leash, there was no way they were getting summoned back to their kennels. Prity sank to her knees as Pinto slapped and swatted her all over her body whilst yelling as many Punjabi expletives as you could effectively cram into twenty seconds. By now, the officers had caught up to her as I struggled to pull her off the battered pulp on the floor at her bare feet. She was reluctantly led off with the assistance of Dalj with her profanities raging on and reaching an ear bashing crescendo. The officers led Prity away in handcuffs for some vital medical work prior to her lonely and long stretch in incarceration, in a dingy rat infested pit in Mumbai's darkest prison.

'Now I know why you did not do this at the hotel. Who would have missed this? Dalj smirked.

Although Pinto had suffered many incidents of ridicule on this weary journey, it was she, who had the last laugh. For behind the zany exterior lay a woman with a whole life time of experiences and hardship, she could smell a wrong un a mile away and the great thing was she never held back, always shooting from her plastic hips at every given moment, and for that we loved her. She possessed more knowledge in her little pinky or browny than some people had eaten steaming meals, she just had a little trouble expressing herself as age had robbed her of her most productive grey cells.

I spoke with officers at the scene and provided statements, my money was returned to me after Baldip explained everything to his brother and I proved my ownership. The carnage that we had witnessed was beginning to clear up and we were given the green light to catch our flight.

Whilst we waited for Baldip to see us off on our return flight home I called Visperal's home telephone number hoping to find out how he was. I spoke to his wife who informed me that he had come out of the coma and the doctors said that he would make a full recovery. She even said that he would be back at the drama school within a matter of weeks. I was so pleased and even more bowled over when she said that Baldip had already phoned earlier and informed them of the news about my successful audition. His wife said that Visperal had every confidence in my ability and wished me all the best and that he was dying to get my autograph now that I had made it, we both laughed and I said that I would see them soon.

Baldip then walked over and with a mere moment to go before we headed off through to our boarding gate. I hugged him as hard as I could muster. He was a friend in the truest sense of the word and I owed him my life. Without him, I would never have known about the skulduggery taking place in the underbelly of my trip. We shook hands firmly and I vowed to come and stay with him when I returned to India filming for '*The Valati*,' and he welcomed me whole heartedly. We boarded the plane, the last three warriors standing, Pinto, Dalj and I, and a short while later the bird took off brushing through the powdery clouds and back home to some much needed sanctity and the rebuilding of my life. I had learnt a valuable insight through the mayhem of the week in that everyone's life is like a Bollywood film. You fall in love; you have your heart broken; you will be involved in arguments; you will have fights; you will be in a love triangle; you will lose loved ones; you will win money; you will lose money; you will have enemies that you make and some that just develop through jealously and other factors. You might even be so lucky to spout the most famous of Bollywood lines, '*Kuta mein tera khoon pi jaaonga*,' - to someone one day, meaning that I will drink your blood you dog! Talking of which, just remember that it is not the size of the dog in the fight, but the size of the fight in the dog, a saying never more apt than it was on this day when my appetite had been voracious. What I did not realise at the time when I had watched that clip from Mukkader Ka Sikkander that day at Dalj's house was that my life would follow the same path as Sikkander in that film and that my girl would actually give her heart to someone else whilst I mopped up the remaining pieces of my life. Above all, I realised that if you put your mind to anything then it can be achieved, I was living proof of that. I made the decision in the aftermath of this watershed trip to allow my spirit to be free from the trivial issues that some people are bogged down with and instead concentrate on what is important – Keeping your loved ones, family, and friends close to your heart, and always being there for them, no matter what. The reality is you really don't know how long you have left with them in this life, so make the most of it!

It seemed that my destiny really had been written as predicted in my 'teva.'
The messianic journey was now over, and this had been my **Rags to Bollywood affair...**

∞∞ Sonny Singh Kalar ∞∞

Printed in the United Kingdom by
Lightning Source UK Ltd., Milton Keynes
141236UK00001B/37/P